Bigfoot 1

Oregon

Mysterious Encounters

Frank Hendersen

Table of Contents

Introduction 3

ENCOUNTER #1 The After Work Encounter 6

ENCOUNTER #2 The Crater Lake Encounter 15

ENCOUNTER #3 The Cooks Encounter 23

ENCOUNTER #4 The Coffee Shop Encounter 32

ENCOUNTER #5 The Elk Hunting Encounter 40

ENCOUNTER #6 The Potato Encounter 50

ENCOUNTER #7 The Truck Stop Encounter 59

ENCOUNTER #8 The Mistaken Identity Encounter 68

ENCOUNTER #9 The Delivery Driver Encounter 76

ENCOUNTER #10 The Bedtime Snack Encounter 84

ENCOUNTER #11 The Road Repair Encounter 92

ENCOUNTER #12 The Trout Encounter 101

ENCOUNTER #13 Orchard Encounter 111

ENCOUNTER #14 The Road Crossing Encounter 120

ENCOUNTER #15 The Teacher's Encounter 129

ENCOUNTER #16 The Dishwasher's Encounter 138

ENCOUNTER #17 The Morning Hike Encounter 147

ENCOUNTER #18 The Lost Dog Encounter 156

ENCOUNTER #19 The Protected Land Encounter 165

ENCOUNTER #20 The Rented Camper Encounter 173

Conclusion 182

Introduction

Embark on a riveting expedition through the untamed wilderness of Oregon, where age-old legends reverberate amidst the bustling cities of Portland and the tranquil serenity of the Cascade Range. Within these pages, we delve into the extraordinary world of Bigfoot encounters in Oregon, offering a fresh and unparalleled perspective on this enduring enigma. As you immerse yourself in this extraordinary odyssey, brace yourself for the mesmerizing accounts of those who claim to have crossed paths with the elusive giant, and let your thoughts wander into the uncharted realms of the age-old question: does Bigfoot truly roam the rugged expanses of Oregon?

Oregon, with its lush forests, meandering rivers, and breathtaking coastline, provides the perfect stage for stories of a creature as mysterious and colossal as Bigfoot. Adding to this captivating setting, Oregon's rich mosaic of indigenous folklore and local myths weaves an intricate tapestry, elevating it as a focal point for narratives that captivate the inquisitive and the skeptical alike. Within these pages, unearth a trove of authentic tales from the Beaver State, each peeling back the layers of mystery that shroud Bigfoot.

However, these stories are not mere diversions; they resonate with the eternal flame of human curiosity and our inherent desire to decode the riddles that confound our comprehension. Whether you're a fervent believer or a prudent skeptic, these accounts are bound to enchant your imagination, compelling you to contemplate our role in the vast mosaic of existence. They promise to evoke a spectrum of emotions, from wonder and introspection to vigilance and reverence, drawing you deeper into the beguiling abyss of the unknown and the tantalizing notion that Bigfoot might truly wander Oregon's hidden domains.

On this voyage, encounter a diverse array of experiences and testimonies, shedding light on the countless individuals who have grappled with the Bigfoot enigma. From urban dwellers to seasoned outdoorsmen, these narratives emanate from individuals just like yourself, forever transformed by their encounters with the inexplicable. These tales are poised to ignite discussions and introspection, urging you to reevaluate your convictions concerning this cryptic denizen of our wilderness.

Prepare yourself for an unparalleled adventure as you navigate the captivating chronicles of Bigfoot encounters in Oregon. Will this expedition bolster your belief in Bigfoot's existence, or will you remain resolute, unmoved by the passionate assertions of witnesses? The answers await within the enthralling narratives contained in this volume.

Take a deep breath and brace yourself for an extraordinary expedition into the heart of mystery. The wonders of Oregon's vast landscapes beckon, and once ensnared by the tales of Bigfoot, your outlook on the world may undergo an irreversible transformation. Are you ready to confront the enigma? The first tale beckons...

ENCOUNTER #1 The After Work Encounter

The drone of hushed conversations filled the air as I stepped into the familiar setting of the shoe store. As the day's weariness weighed on my shoulders, I glanced around, noting the faces of regulars, and new customers browsing through the aisles. It had been a routine day at school, but my job here, where I'd worked for over a year, was always unpredictable.

The golden afternoon light slanted through the windows, casting playful patterns on the wooden floor. From a corner of the store, an old radio played soft melodies, creating an atmosphere that felt detached from the bustling world outside. My coworkers smiled as they assisted customers, their friendly exchanges painting the air with familiarity.

I clocked in, adjusting my store badge that read "Sarah, at your service." Although I was only 17, I had mastered the art of picking the perfect pair of shoes for anyone, which made me a favorite among our patrons. The constant hum of activity always took my mind off school stress, at least for a while.

The morning sun had greeted me with its usual warmth as I rushed through school corridors. The weight of the backpack was nothing compared to the load of pending assignments and deadlines. Every classroom seemed to echo with the same urgency, teachers handing out more work, and students groaning in response.

During lunch, I had stolen a moment with my friends. We sat under the big oak tree, its leaves rustling softly in the wind. Our conversations varied, from the newest movie releases to the mysteries of algebra. However, the shadow of my incomplete homework loomed in the back of my mind.

By the time the final bell rang, it felt as though the day had stretched on for years. The school's clock tower chimed, its somber tone marking the end of another long day. With heavy steps, I made my way out, anticipating the evening rush at the shoe store.

Back at the shoe store, I slid into my role with practiced ease. Customers flowed in and out, each with a unique request or story to tell. A little girl wanted pink ballerina shoes; an elderly man needed something for his evening walks.

Amidst the organized chaos, I felt a connection with every individual. Their stories and their smiles made the hours fly by. With each shoebox I handed over, I imagined the journeys those shoes would take, the steps they'd mark in someone's life.

The evening seemed to whirl by in a series of shoe laces, leather, and laughter. The clock soon struck 8:30 pm. The once radiant sun was now setting, painting the sky with hues of gold and crimson. It was time for me to head home, but the universe had other plans.

The cool evening breeze was a gentle caress as I began my drive home. The familiar path took me alongside a vast open field, its grass swaying in rhythm with the wind. On the opposite side, a dense forest stood tall, its trees holding secrets of ages gone by.

The setting sun, now a fiery ball on the horizon, cast its golden glow on everything. My old car hummed softly, its headlights piercing through the gathering twilight. As I drove, my thoughts were consumed by the day's events, and the unfinished homework waiting for me.

Suddenly, a movement at the edge of the field caught my attention. My heart raced as my eyes tried to discern what lurked in the dim light. Something was out there, and it was unlike anything I'd ever seen.

Two massive figures walked alongside the field, their steps in sync with my car's slow pace. From this distance, it was hard to tell if they were human or something else. Their tall silhouettes seemed to sway with the wind, casting long, haunting shadows that danced with the dimming daylight.

Curiosity welled up inside me, urging me to slow down further. The figures' features were hidden, but their sheer size made them stand out. My mind raced, trying to decipher if they were a trick of the light or if my tired eyes were playing games with me.

A chill ran down my spine as I continued to watch. There was something otherworldly about these beings, something that defied explanation. And as the distance between us closed, I felt a tug of mystery pulling me deeper into their enigma.

Drawing closer, every detail of these enigmatic beings became clearer. They moved with an uncanny grace, their feet barely touching the ground. Their long, unkempt hair flowed like waves, hiding most of their features. Yet, beneath those tangled locks, glimpses of their faces peeked through.

The closer I got, the more certain I became that these figures were not ordinary humans. Their sheer size was intimidating, but it was the aura around them that felt truly alien. Everything about them radiated an energy that was palpable, filling the evening air with an indescribable tension.

Their eyes, though mostly hidden, seemed to glow with a faint luminescence. They watched me with an intensity that was both captivating and terrifying. Each step they took felt deliberate, as if every movement was part of a dance only they understood.

I gripped the steering wheel tighter, trying to make sense of what I was witnessing. The logical part of my mind screamed that these creatures shouldn't exist, that they were a figment of my tired imagination. But every instinct told me that they were real, and they were not from this world.

It wasn't just their appearance; it was the way they moved, the air around them, the energy they emitted. It all pointed to something beyond my understanding. I felt a mixture of wonder and dread, captivated by their presence, yet fearful of their intentions.

Questions raced through my mind. Were they benign visitors or harbingers of something more sinister? Had anyone else seen them, or was I the only witness to this strange phenomenon? With every passing second, the weight of the mystery grew heavier.

Finally, my neighborhood came into view, pulling me from my trance. The familiarity of the houses and streets offered a brief respite from the unsettling encounter. I drove into my driveway, my car's engine breaking the silence of the night.

Stepping out, I was greeted by the warm glow of our porch light. The front door opened, revealing my mom's comforting face. Her cheerful greeting and the scent of home-cooked food momentarily pushed away the eerie memories of the drive.

However, even in the safety of my home, the shadows of the creatures loomed large in my mind. As I shared casual exchanges with my family, the contrast between the normalcy of home and the strangeness of the encounter became even starker.

I retreated to the sanctuary of my room, trying to process everything. The soft glow of my desk lamp illuminated the scattered sheets of homework, but my concentration was elsewhere. The plate of lasagna sat untouched, my appetite lost to the day's mysteries.

Could it be that I had stumbled upon something no one else had seen? Or was it possible that others had witnessed these creatures but chose to remain silent? The uncertainty gnawed at me, and the solitude of my room amplified my confusion.

I gazed out of my window, searching the night sky for answers. The stars twinkled back, their age-old light providing no clarity. The enigma of the beings remained, filling my thoughts and leaving me with more questions than answers.

Years flew by, but the memory of that evening refused to fade. Every now and then, when the world around me grew silent and my thoughts wandered, I would find myself back on that road, with those immense beings looming in the distance. Their presence had left an indelible mark on my psyche.

Life progressed, filled with its usual ups and downs. I graduated, went to college, and began building my life. Friends came and went, experiences piled up, and yet, in quiet moments, the echo of that evening would return. The question of who or what they were never ceased to intrigue me.

I never spoke of the incident to anyone, not even my closest friends. The fear of disbelief or ridicule held me back. But deep inside, I always hoped to find someone who had seen what I had, someone who could share in the mystery and wonder of that inexplicable evening.

ENCOUNTER #2 The Crater Lake Encounter

The open road seemed to stretch infinitely before us, promising adventures unknown. It had been two days since our last significant stop at Mount Rushmore, a place of sheer historical awe. The giant stone faces seemed to whisper stories from the past as we stood before them, feeling utterly dwarfed.

From there, the Grand Canyon had beckoned. The vast chasm seemed like a world of its own, holding deep secrets. My brother, Brett, had playfully shouted into the abyss, laughing as our voices echoed back, intertwining with the whispers of ancient times.

As morning rays peaked into our hotel room today, there was a shared, unspoken excitement. The agenda was Crater Lake National Park. I could already imagine the pristine waters reflecting the sky, but little did we know what awaited us.

Upon reaching Crater Lake National Park, a world of vibrant greens and a symphony of bird calls welcomed us. The trails beckoned, winding mysteriously into dense woods. My mom, Emily, was especially fascinated by the local flora, frequently pausing to admire them.

Each flower she found seemed to hold a story of its own, from the bright blues that mirrored the lake to the deep purples that seemed to hide shadows within. I could see her lost in thought, perhaps contemplating the tales they held, tales older than any of us.

Brett and Jordan, though usually distracted by their games, couldn't help but stop every once in a while, drawn into nature's allure. Their playful banter seemed subdued, replaced by a rare, reflective silence.

The trail opened up, revealing the serene Crater Lake. Its waters, crystal clear, mirrored the sky with an accuracy that was almost eerie. A distant island in the lake caught our attention, appearing as if floating on clouds reflected in the water.

We settled down by the lake's edge, feeling its calm wash over us. Mom handed out granola bars, and for a while, the only sounds were the soft crunch of our snacks and the gentle ripple of water.

Yet, the tranquility was soon broken by Jordan's curious voice, "What's that over there?" We all turned, trying to discern what had caught his attention in the dense woods to our left.

The atmosphere shifted as we all felt it - the peculiar sensation of being watched. While the logical side of me echoed Dad's assurances about the local wildlife, the steady, two-footed sound of footsteps suggested otherwise. The forest suddenly seemed more imposing, its depths more profound.

Brett, never one to shy away from a mystery, inched closer to the source of the noise. His beckoning gestures spoke of something extraordinary, so, one by one, we followed, our footsteps syncing with the mysterious rhythm from the woods.

As we peered deeper into the forest's embrace, the sunlight filtering through the leaves played tricks on our eyes. Shadows danced, taking forms both familiar and strange, making our hearts race with a mix of excitement and fear.

Just when I thought it was my imagination, there it was - a massive, obscured figure moving with purpose. It seemed to blend with the trees yet stood out due to its sheer size. Its movements were fluid, echoing a primal dance with nature.

Moments felt stretched as we caught a brief, yet clear, sight of the creature. Covered in dark, coarse hair, its height was astonishing. And the face – it was eerily human-like, yet wild. The deep-set eyes, filled with wisdom, briefly met ours before the creature continued on its path.

The world around seemed to pause, the birds quiet, and the wind still. We were left in stunned silence, the weight of what we'd witnessed pressing down on us. Was it the legend the locals spoke of? The guardian of the lake? Only time would tell.

Returning to our spot by the serene lake, the calm surroundings were in stark contrast to the storm of emotions inside us. The rhythmic sound of the water helped ground our racing hearts. For a moment, we all sat, letting the weight of what we'd witnessed settle in.

Brett, never one to hold back, broke the silence, "We just saw Bigfoot, didn't we?" His words, though filled with excitement, carried a hint of disbelief. We all exchanged glances, our faces mirroring the same thought.

The legend, the stories we'd heard of a guardian spirit of the forest, all seemed more real now. With every step forward on our hike, we were more alert, listening keenly to every rustle, every whisper of the woods.

The mysterious aura of the forest had intensified. What once was a casual hike had transformed into a journey of keen observation. Every shadow, every distant sound now had us guessing. Was it another creature? Was it watching us?

Jordan and Brett started to playfully challenge each other on who would spot another unusual phenomenon first. Their usual antics had a new flavor, a mix of excitement and curiosity, punctuated by bursts of laughter and gasps.

Though we tried to continue our hike as before, the forest's mystery had consumed us. We became detectives of nature, each corner, each turn holding a promise of another enigma.

As the day wore on, the sun started its descent, casting a golden hue on everything. It was time to leave this enchanted place and head back to our trusty van. The path back seemed different, every tree, every rock now held a story.

Reaching the parking lot, the sight of other families and hikers was oddly reassuring. The familiar sounds of car doors, laughter, and distant chatter made the world seem normal again.

Yet, as we climbed into our van, the boys' eyes sparkled with the secrets of the forest. Their whispers and excited recollections were a testament to the day's extraordinary events.

The engine's hum was a gentle reminder that our road trip was far from over. As the scenery changed, the boys, instead of retreating into the digital world of their phones, kept their eyes glued to the windows.

Every dense cluster of trees, every shadowy patch now held the promise of another sighting. Their animated discussions, theories, and recounts of our encounter with the unknown filled the van.

While I navigated the winding roads, Emily's hand found mine, giving it a reassuring squeeze. The unspoken words between us were clear: this trip had turned into an unexpected adventure, one that would be retold for years to come.

As the day ended and the first stars appeared, a sense of wonder enveloped us. The boys debated whether to share our incredible encounter with the world or keep it as our little secret.

Deep in thought, I considered the implications. Sharing our story could lead to disbelief, ridicule, or worse, harm the creature in its natural habitat. Weighing the pros and cons, I finally spoke, suggesting we cherish this as a family memory.

With the vast expanse of the open road ahead, our journey took on a new dimension. The boys, energized and curious, eagerly looked out, hoping for another brush with the mystical. Our road trip had become a quest, an expedition into the heart of the unknown.

ENCOUNTER #3 The Cooks Encounter

As I drove my trusty truck down the winding Oregon roads, the tall trees seemed to lean in, almost like they were whispering secrets to each other. I had chosen to spend my short vacation camping, hoping to find a bit of peace away from my busy life as a cook. The sun dappled through the dense canopy, painting golden patterns on the road. Oregon was my home, and I knew its forests like the back of my hand, but this particular area was new to me.

Thinking back, my life had its ups and downs. A marriage that lasted just a year in my twenties seemed like a distant memory now. We never had kids, which, looking back, felt like a good thing. Since then, solitude felt right, as if I was meant to walk some paths alone.

The campsite came into view, nestled amidst the towering trees. Something about this spot felt different. An eerie stillness hung in the air, making the hairs on the back of my neck stand up. I shook off the strange feeling and began to unload my gear, ready to set up camp.

As I pegged down my tent, a faint rustling caught my attention. I turned, scanning the surrounding woods, but saw nothing. Maybe it was just a squirrel or a bird, I reasoned. Yet, the dense forest seemed to hide more than it revealed, and a mysterious chill ran down my spine.

With my tent set up, I decided to stretch my legs. Walking amidst the trees, I felt both dwarfed and protected. Every now and then, the silence was broken by distant bird calls or the rustling of leaves underfoot. The forest felt alive, watching and waiting.

Soon, the light started to fade, urging me to head back to the campsite. The setting sun painted the sky in shades of pink and orange, providing a beautiful backdrop to the darkening woods. As night began to claim the forest, I felt a mix of excitement and unease.

Back at camp, the first order of business was dinner. I took pride in my culinary skills, and tonight, I was set on making a gourmet meal over the open fire. I could almost taste the perfectly grilled meat, the roasted vegetables, and the hint of smoky flavor that the fire would lend them.

As I cooked, the soft chirping of crickets and the distant hooting of an owl accompanied me. It felt peaceful, with the fire's warmth chasing away the growing cold. But as I settled down to enjoy my meal, a soft knocking sound echoed through the woods. It was distant, yet unmistakable.

I paused, straining my ears. The rhythmic wood knocking continued for a few minutes, and then, as abruptly as it had started, it stopped. A bit unnerved, I decided it must be someone chopping wood at another campsite. Trying to shake off the unsettling feeling, I lay back, watching the stars shimmer above.

The next morning, a soft glow seeped into my tent. I rose, stretching and taking a deep breath of the fresh, cool air. Determined to make the most of my day, I decided to start with a hearty breakfast. I could already smell the aroma of sizzling bacon and fresh coffee.

With breakfast done, I took a leisurely walk. The forest was bathed in sunlight, making everything seem brighter and more alive. Birds chirped overhead, and the distant sound of running water hinted at a stream or river nearby. Lost in the beauty around me, I almost didn't notice the strange markings on a tree trunk.

They looked like deep gashes, as if something sharp had scraped the bark off. Intrigued, I followed the markings, which seemed to lead deeper into the woods. But as the path grew denser and the markings more frequent, a nagging voice in my head suggested it might be better to turn back.

The day progressed peacefully. I read a bit, enjoyed my lunch, and even took a short nap. But as evening approached, so did the unease. The forest seemed to darken faster than usual, and once again, I began to prepare my dinner over the open fire.

Just as I was about to take my first bite, the knocking sound returned. This time, it was louder, closer. It echoed through the stillness, creating a rhythm that was almost hypnotic. I stood still, every sense alert, trying to locate the source.

From the edge of the clearing, a shadow emerged. At first, it was hard to make out any details, but as it moved closer, its form became clearer. Tall, covered in thick fur, it moved gracefully, yet with a sense of power. My heart raced as I realized I wasn't alone. The mystery of the woods was unfolding before me.

The creature's eyes, deep and penetrating, studied me intently. Its fur was a mix of dark brown and black, giving it an almost camouflage-like appearance against the forest backdrop. The face was eerily human, yet distinctly different – broad nose, deep-set eyes, and an expression of genuine curiosity.

There we stood, man and beast, mere feet apart, silently observing one another. Its massive frame was muscular, yet it moved with a gentle ease. The realization hit me like a ton of bricks. I was face to face with Bigfoot, the legendary creature of the Pacific Northwest. Stories and rumors had circled for years, but I never believed them, until now.

Without any warning, the creature turned and slowly walked back into the dense woods, its large footprints leaving a trace in the soft earth. I was left in stunned silence, trying to process what I had just witnessed. The air seemed to pulse with an unspoken understanding: this was its home, and I was merely a visitor.

With the creature gone, the atmosphere around the camp felt altered. Every small sound was amplified, and the weight of the encounter pressed down on me. I considered packing up and heading home, but a strange calmness held me in place. The creature didn't seem to mean me any harm; it was just as curious about me as I was about it.

As the night deepened, I sat by the fire, reflecting on the past, my short-lived marriage, and my solitary life. Perhaps, in some ways, the creature and I were similar – both solitary beings, making our way through the vast wilderness of life.

Despite the evening's unexpected visitor, sleep came surprisingly easy. The rhythmic sounds of the forest acted as a lullaby, and I drifted off, the mysterious wood knocking fading into the distance.

Morning arrived, bringing with it a new sense of purpose. The events of the previous night replayed in my mind as I packed up my camp. The forest seemed to whisper its secrets, and I felt more connected to nature than ever before.

As I loaded up my truck, the forest felt different, as if it had shared one of its most profound secrets with me. The dense trees, the shimmering streams, and even the birdsong seemed to resonate with the memory of last night.

The drive back home was contemplative. The winding roads, the hills, and the open skies seemed to hold new meaning. The world was filled with wonders, and I had just experienced one of its most elusive mysteries.

Returning to work that evening, the bustling restaurant felt like a different world. The noise, the lights, and the chatter seemed miles away from the serenity of the woods. As I cooked and served, my mind often wandered back to the encounter.

Conversations swirled around me, but I kept my incredible experience to myself. Who would believe me, anyway? Still, as I moved through the restaurant, I found myself scanning faces, wondering if any of them had had a similar encounter.

The night went on, dishes coming and going, laughter and music filling the air. Yet, amidst all the chaos, a peaceful thought lingered in my mind. I had experienced something truly special, and nothing could take that away.

The weeks that followed were filled with a mix of routine and reflection. The forest called to me, and I often found myself returning to that same campsite, hoping for another glimpse of the mysterious creature.

Though I never saw Bigfoot again, the strange knocking sounds occasionally echoed through the trees, a gentle reminder of our shared moment. It felt like a nod of acknowledgment, a signal that said, "I'm still here."

Life went on, but the memory of that encounter remained fresh, a beacon of wonder in the everyday grind. And as I lay in bed each night, the vast Oregon wilderness outside, I took comfort in the thought that out there, amidst the tall trees, magic was real.

ENCOUNTER #4 The Coffee Shop Encounter

Ever since I was a kid, the deep aroma of coffee seemed like magic to me. I'd sit on the kitchen counter, swinging my legs, watching Mom and Dad sip their morning brew. The comfort and warmth of those moments stayed with me as I grew older.

Living in Oregon, you couldn't miss the tiny drive-through coffee stands everywhere. They were like little huts, sprinkled across towns and highways. It felt like a unique world, where coffee was the hero, and I knew I wanted to be a part of it.

When I finally took the leap and opened my coffee shop, things weren't as rosy as I imagined. My savings went into setting it up, and the stress kept me up many nights. With a young daughter and a supportive wife, the stakes were high. But I believed in the dream, and that belief pushed me every day.

The early months were hard. I'd watch other drive-throughs always buzzing with customers while mine stood mostly silent. But giving up wasn't an option. I tweaked my coffee blend, trying to perfect it, until one day, a regular said it was the best he ever had.

Word began to spread, slowly but surely. The mornings became busier, and soon there was a line of cars waiting. It felt like a dream. My wife, Maria, would often join me, and together, we'd handle the morning rush.

Our daughter, Lucy, became the shop's little mascot. Customers would wave at her, and she'd giggle from her little corner, playing with her toys. With time, our struggles started to fade, and the sound of laughter and coffee beans grinding filled the air.

Weekday mornings required an early start. The sky would still be painted in shades of twilight as I pulled into the shop's parking lot. The cold Oregon air would sting my face, but the thought of the first pot of coffee kept me going.

By sunrise, the aroma of fresh coffee would drift into the air, drawing in folks from all around. It was like a magnet, pulling in both the early birds heading to work and the wanderers just starting their day.

The location of the shop was its hidden treasure. On the town's edge, it was a perfect stop. Local folks driving to work, tourists heading out for adventures, all found their way to my little coffee haven.

The drive-through window was like a portal to countless stories. There was Mr. Hansen, always in a hurry, grabbing his double espresso. Then there was Rose, an elderly lady who'd order a cappuccino and always had a new tale to share about her grandchildren.

Tourists often stumbled upon the shop. Curious and excited, they'd ask for local recommendations. I'd often chat with them, sharing secrets of the town, and in return, they'd tell me about their hometowns or adventures. It felt like I was traveling the world without ever leaving my shop.

My favorite part was the banter. Quick jokes, shared stories, and the hum of daily life made every day special. The drive-through wasn't just a window for coffee; it was a window to life's many stories.

One particular morning, something felt off. The air had a mysterious chill, and there was an odd silence. As I parked my car, a rustling sound near the garbage cans caught my attention. Squinting in the dim light, I saw a shadowy figure that seemed larger than any animal I knew.

The figure swiftly disappeared behind some bushes before I could get a closer look. My heart raced. Bears were not common here, and it seemed too large for a dog. Shaking off the eerie feeling, I convinced myself it was probably just a stray animal.

The day progressed as usual. The morning rush, the laughter, the stories, all felt normal. But in the back of my mind, the mysterious shadow lingered. Every time I looked towards the garbage cans, I couldn't help but wonder about the strange visitor from the morning.

Afternoons at the shop were usually quieter. With the morning rush over, I found a few moments to breathe and take care of other duties. As the clock struck 2pm, I began clearing up some trash, planning to dump it out back.

As I approached the garbage cans, something on the ground caught my eye. There, imprinted in the soft gravel, were two massive footprints. They were unlike anything I'd ever seen. Far too big to be human, but too distinct to be just any animal's.

A shiver ran down my spine. These footprints were eerily detailed, showing clear toe patterns and a deep impression, as if something heavy had stood there. Pushing away my initial fear, I decided to get a second opinion on what could've made these prints.

I called out to James, a young college guy who worked part-time with me. He was always curious about things and had a knack for solving puzzles. "Hey, James," I beckoned, "You gotta see this."

His eyes widened the moment he saw the footprints. We both stared in silence, trying to make sense of it. "You know," James finally broke the silence, "this looks like... no, it couldn't be... like a Bigfoot's footprint." He seemed half-joking, but his face betrayed a genuine bewilderment.

I had heard tales of Bigfoot, especially growing up in the Pacific Northwest. Every camping trip or night around a bonfire would have someone sharing a spooky Bigfoot story. I always dismissed them as mere tales, but now, staring at the footprints, I wasn't so sure.

Paragraph 1: James and I retreated inside the shop, our minds racing with thoughts of the legendary creature. James began to share stories his grandparents told him, of strange sightings and eerie sounds in the woods. Tales that always ended with a whispered mention of Bigfoot.

As he spoke, memories of my own childhood tales returned. Campfire stories of the elusive creature, footprints found in the middle of nowhere, and even blurry photos that some claimed were the real deal. Though I'd never really believed them, the stories now felt all too real.

The afternoon crowd started trickling in, and we tried to act normal. But our conversations kept drifting back to the mystery outside. Every creak of the door or rustle of leaves made us jump, half-expecting to see the creature from the legends.

News travels fast in small towns. By late afternoon, word had gotten around about the strange footprints at my coffee shop. The drive-through, which usually slowed by this time, was now buzzing with curious folks from all over town.

Some came to laugh it off, calling it a prank. Others seemed genuinely intrigued, discussing their own encounters or stories they'd heard. The air was filled with excitement, skepticism, and a hint of fear.

Cameras flashed as people took photos of the footprints. Some even tried to place their own feet next to the prints, highlighting the vast size difference. My little coffee shop had become the epicenter of the town's latest mystery.

As evening approached, the crowd began to thin. I sat at one of the tables, a cup of coffee in hand, lost in thought. The events of the day seemed surreal. The shop was back to its familiar hum, but the atmosphere felt charged with mystery.

I gazed out of the window, the setting sun casting long shadows. The silhouette of the bushes where I had seen the mysterious figure in the morning looked eerily beautiful. Despite the chaos of the day, there was a strange peace in that moment.

Whether Bigfoot was real or just a tale, I knew today would be a story I'd tell for years. I felt connected to the legends in a way I never had before. As darkness took over, I couldn't help but wonder if the creature might visit again.

ENCOUNTER #5 The Elk Hunting Encounter

The morning sun peeked through the curtains of our hotel room in Oregon, filling the room with golden light. I yawned and stretched, excited about another day of elk hunting with my best friend, Bill. We'd been doing this since our high school days, and every trip felt like a mini-adventure. This trip, however, was extra special because Bill had just bought a shiny new rifle that he was eager to show off.

Bill unpacked his new rifle, grinning from ear to ear. "Look at this beauty, Todd," he exclaimed, handing it over to me. The weight felt good in my hands, and the polished metal glinted in the sunlight. I teased him, saying, "Better not miss any shots this time!" We both laughed, remembering past hunts where Bill's aim wasn't quite on target.

After a hearty breakfast at the hotel's diner, we headed out. We had a routine each morning: drive to the gravel parking lot next to the public hunting land, then hike into the vast Oregon wilderness. Oregon was known for its massive elks, and we always dreamt of spotting one. But elk hunting wasn't easy. The dense woods and hilly terrain often tested our patience and skills.

As we began our hike, memories from our school days flooded back. Borrowed cars, saving pennies for ammunition, and our shared dreams of landing a trophy elk. We walked in comfortable silence, the weight of our gear on our backs and the soft crunch of leaves under our boots. The air was crisp, and the scent of pine filled our nostrils.

We had been in these woods for a few days now, scouting and hoping. Some days we saw signs of elk, like tracks or droppings, but they were always just out of sight. The thrill of the hunt was in the chase, but it could also be draining, especially when the elks seemed to always be one step ahead.

Bill, ever the optimist, chirped, "Today's the day, I can feel it!" His optimism was infectious, and I couldn't help but smile. "With your new rifle in tow, how could we miss?" I replied. But as the hours rolled by, our earlier enthusiasm waned slightly, replaced by a quiet determination.

By afternoon, we chose a strategic spot atop a ridgeline, overlooking a quiet valley. We had a clear view of the area below, ideal for spotting any movement. I set up a small camp: a tarp for shade, some snacks, and our binoculars. The sun was high in the sky, and a gentle breeze cooled our faces.

Suddenly, a rustling sound caught our attention. I grabbed my binoculars, scanning the valley, and there she was: a female elk, majestic and graceful. "There's one," Bill whispered, excitement clear in his voice. But our hopes dropped when we realized it was a female. Hunting laws prohibited shooting her.

We watched, captivated, as she moved along the valley floor. Even though we couldn't shoot, seeing an elk up close in its natural environment was a treat. We shared a silent moment of appreciation, snapping pictures and making quiet observations. Little did we know, the real spectacle was yet to come.

The elk suddenly stopped, her ears perking up. She seemed tense, looking back towards the bushes from where she'd come. Bill and I exchanged confused glances. What had startled her? Then, a second rustling, louder and more pronounced, echoed through the valley.

Before we could react, an enormous creature emerged from the foliage. It was unlike anything we'd ever seen, standing over nine feet tall, with thick, dark fur. Its face was eerily human, with deep-set eyes that held an intelligent, mysterious glint. My heart raced, every instinct telling me this wasn't just another woodland animal.

The creature, which looked like the legendary Bigfoot, bolted after the elk. The valley erupted in chaos. The speed of the chase was astonishing. The elk, now in a desperate bid for survival, tried to outrun the creature. And as the chase moved further away from our vantage point, Bill and I were left in stunned silence, our minds struggling to comprehend what we had just witnessed.

We remained motionless for what felt like hours, trying to process the surreal event. Neither of us dared to speak, the weight of the moment heavy in the air. Every sound, every movement in the forest now seemed amplified, as if the woods were whispering secrets.

Bill broke the silence, his voice quivering, "Did we...did we just see Bigfoot?" I nodded slowly, just as unsure as he was. The stories we'd heard growing up, tales of the mysterious creature lurking in these woods, suddenly felt all too real. The fear was palpable, but so was the excitement. We had witnessed something truly extraordinary.

As the sun began its descent, casting long shadows across the valley, we decided to head back to the hotel. The forest, once familiar and comforting, now felt eerie and unpredictable. We walked briskly, every rustling leaf or snapping twig causing us to jump. By the time we reached the gravel parking lot, night had almost set in, and we were grateful for the safety of our car.

The car's engine hummed softly as we drove back to the hotel, the headlights piercing the inky darkness. The radio played softly in the background, but neither of us was really listening. The night seemed to press in on us from all sides, and the forest, once a place of adventure, now felt like a place of hidden dangers.

Bill finally spoke, trying to lighten the mood, "Well, that was interesting." I chuckled nervously, appreciating his attempt to break the tension. "Interesting? That's one way to put it," I replied. But beneath our banter was an unspoken agreement - what we saw would stay between us. There was no telling how others might react to our story.

The bright lights of the hotel were a welcome sight. We parked and hurried inside, eager for the familiarity and comfort of our room. The lobby was empty, save for the night clerk who gave us a friendly nod. We returned the gesture, but our minds were elsewhere, replaying the day's events.

Inside our room, we dumped our gear and settled onto our beds. The room was quiet, save for the gentle hum of the air conditioner. I looked over at Bill, who was staring at the ceiling, lost in thought. The weight of the day's discovery weighed heavily on both of us.

"We should talk about it," I began, "About what we saw." Bill nodded slowly, sitting up. "I've heard stories, you know? About Bigfoot sightings in these woods. But I never truly believed them until now." His eyes held a mixture of fear and wonder. We began to discuss the creature in detail, trying to make sense of its appearance, its actions, and its incredible speed.

The hours ticked by as we shared our thoughts, sometimes in excited whispers, other times in hushed tones. We pondered on whether we should continue hunting the next day or cut our trip short. After a lengthy debate, the decision was unanimous: perhaps it was best to leave in the morning. Safety, after all, was paramount.

We woke up the next morning, the previous day's events feeling almost dreamlike. As we packed our bags, there was a palpable sense of relief in the air. The woods and its mysteries could wait for another day, another time. Right now, heading home felt like the right choice.

We grabbed a quick breakfast from the hotel's diner, our conversation centered on mundane topics - the weather, the drive back, and plans for the next few days. But every so often, our gaze would drift, lost in thought, remembering the creature and the chase.

As we pulled out of the hotel's parking lot, the dense Oregon forest stretched out on either side of the road. The towering trees and thick underbrush hid a world of secrets. We were leaving with more questions than answers, but there was one thing we both knew for sure: we had a story to tell, even if we chose to keep it to ourselves.

The drive home was filled with stretches of silence, each of us lost in our own thoughts. The vast landscape of Oregon rolled by, the dense forests giving way to open fields and then back to woods again. The beauty of the state was undeniable, but it now held a new layer of mystery for us.

Bill finally broke the silence. "Do you think it saw us?" he mused, glancing at me. I pondered the question for a moment. "I don't know," I admitted. "But if it did, it didn't seem interested in us. It was focused on the elk." We both shuddered, recalling the intensity of the chase.

We chatted about other Bigfoot stories we'd heard over the years, trying to piece together any similarities or patterns. Every tale seemed to have its own unique elements, but one thing remained consistent: the feeling of awe and fear experienced by those who encountered the creature.

As we neared our hometown, the familiarity of the surroundings was comforting. The wild, untamed landscapes of the hunting grounds felt worlds away. Pulling into my driveway, we unloaded the gear, the weight of our equipment now matched by the weight of our shared secret.

We said our goodbyes, but before Bill drove off, he turned to me, a serious look on his face. "We don't have to tell anyone," he said. "But we'll always have this memory, this bond." I nodded in agreement, grateful for our friendship and the unspoken understanding between us.

As I watched his car disappear down the road, I took a deep breath, letting the cool Oregon air fill my lungs. The house was quiet when I entered, and I found comfort in its familiar walls and rooms. But as I settled into bed that night, the image of the creature kept replaying in my mind. Its size, its speed, and its uncanny intelligence left an indelible mark on my memory.

ENCOUNTER #6 The Potato Encounter

The woods around my Oregon home had always been my refuge. They offered peace and quiet, a haven from the rest of the world. I remembered how my dear husband and I built this home together, how we cherished every brick, every beam, and how the tall trees whispered tales of love to us.

Now, living alone after he passed away, every corner of our home brought back memories. The morning sun streamed through the trees, casting dancing shadows on my garden, where a mix of vegetables thrived. It was a crisp morning, and the scents from the blooms brought back shared moments, days of laughter, and nights of shared dreams.

But lately, the solitude of the forest was broken by eerie howls. They were distant, yet powerful enough to rattle my thoughts. It wasn't like any animal I knew of. The sounds would linger in the air, making the woods feel more mysterious than ever.

Each morning, as I watered my vegetable patch, memories of our shared life enveloped me. The tomatoes glistened with dew, the carrots stood tall, and the potatoes, our first joint project, lay buried, waiting for harvest. They were our babies, since we never had children of our own.

Today, as I hummed an old tune, I felt the same autumn wind that would often prompt my husband to wrap a shawl around me. The forest felt alive, the leaves rustled, and the familiar chirping of the birds kept me company. But the tranquillity was once again shattered by that mysterious howl. It felt closer this time, adding to the growing intrigue.

Was there another creature out there? I pondered over the howls. Perhaps an animal in distress? Or maybe, just maybe, the forest had more secrets than I had ever imagined.

After a morning in the garden, I decided to prepare myself a hearty lunch. I picked the ripest potatoes, thinking of how my husband used to adore my potato salad. Peeling them on my back porch, I felt a comforting connection with nature and the past.

As I got lost in the rhythm of peeling, a sudden rustle snapped me out of my trance. It was louder than the usual squirrel mischief or the playful birds. My heart raced as I squinted into the dense woods, trying to locate the source of the disturbance.

In a fleeting moment, between the shadows of the trees, I thought I saw movement. The outline was too big to be any regular forest dweller. Could it be the source of the mysterious howls? My thoughts raced, and curiosity surged within me.

Clutching the potato peeler, I stood still, my senses heightened. The sun's rays pierced through the canopy, and there it was, an unfamiliar creature. The sight was partial, but what I saw was unlike anything I had ever seen. Its face appeared almost human, with deep-set eyes that seemed to be studying me.

Its nose was broad and flat, and its jaw jutted out slightly. The skin looked rough, and the wrinkles on its face told tales of age. A blend of curiosity and intelligence shone in its gaze, almost as if it was as intrigued by me as I was by it.

Time seemed to slow as we locked eyes. The creature then began to move, revealing its towering stature. I saw glimpses of its body covered in coarse hair before it retreated, blending into the woods. As suddenly as it had appeared, it vanished, leaving behind only an aura of mystery.

As the reality of what I witnessed began to sink in, the forest was filled with a resonating howl. The powerful sound seemed to come from the very spot the creature had vanished. It felt like a call, an announcement, or perhaps a signal to others of its kind.

Shaken but intrigued, I gathered my courage and decided to investigate. Approaching the spot, I noticed a faint trail. It looked recent, possibly made by the creature itself. The forest floor was disturbed, showing signs of its massive footprints.

My heart thudded loudly in my chest. Was I truly ready to uncover the forest's secrets? I decided to follow the trail a short distance. The footprints led me further into the woods before they disappeared, leaving me with more questions than answers. The howls, the creature, the footprints – were they all connected?

The following day, the creature's face was still vivid in my mind. Was it hungry? Lost? Curious about me? I thought about our brief encounter, and an idea took root. Maybe, just maybe, I could leave out some food, a peace offering or a gesture of friendship.

I gathered some vegetables, the leftover potato salad, and some bread. I took them to the spot on the trail where I had seen the creature. I neatly arranged them on a large leaf, leaving it as a humble offering. As I retraced my steps, I hoped that the creature would find the food and understand my gesture.

It became a silent ritual. Every morning, I would visit the trail, and every day the food would be gone. There were no signs of who or what took it, but I felt a silent connection forming. It was like an unspoken agreement, an understanding between two beings from different worlds.

Two weeks went by, and the routine continued. I'd leave the food, and by the next morning, it would vanish. I never saw the creature again, but I felt its presence. The forest felt different, alive in a new way. The mysterious bond we shared was strange yet comforting.

I often wondered if it watched me from the shadows, curious about the old woman who left gifts in its path. Maybe it was grateful or perhaps puzzled. Either way, our silent pact felt like a small bridge, connecting two vastly different lives.

Each offering was like sending out a message in a bottle, hoping it would be found and understood. It wasn't just about the food. It was about reaching out, trying to understand, and hoping to be understood.

One morning, as the sun cast its golden hues on the forest floor, I approached the trail with my usual offering. However, to my surprise, the previous day's food lay untouched. Birds chirped around, but the scene felt unusually still. My heart sank a little; what could have changed?

I thought maybe the creature wasn't hungry or perhaps found food elsewhere. I decided to leave the food there and added a bit more, hoping it would return. Maybe it was just a fluke, and everything would be back to our familiar routine by tomorrow.

But the next morning brought the same sight. The food remained untouched, the forest was silent, and there was no sign of the creature. A sinking feeling settled in my chest. Had the creature moved on? Or had something happened to it?

Days turned into nights, and the food I left on the trail remained undisturbed. Each evening, as the sun painted the sky with shades of orange and pink, I'd sit on my porch, lost in thought. The mysterious creature, with its deep eyes and curious gaze, had left an indelible mark on my life.

I began to accept that perhaps our brief interaction was over. Maybe it had found a new home or another food source. Or perhaps it wanted to avoid any more human contact. My heart felt heavy, but there was also a sense of gratitude.

I was thankful for the moments of wonder it brought into my otherwise quiet life. It reminded me of the countless mysteries the world holds, the unseen stories, and the silent connections we share with beings we might never fully understand.

Time moved on, and the forest resumed its usual rhythm. The howls that once echoed mysteriously through the trees ceased, leaving behind only memories. My days returned to their usual routine of tending to my garden, reading my books, and reminiscing about the past.

Yet, the experience with the creature changed something within me. It added a layer of magic to the woods I called home, a tale I could share, and a memory to cherish. I often found myself wandering to that trail, hoping to catch a glimpse or hear a distant howl.

As days turned into weeks and then months, I never heard or saw the creature again. But its presence left a lasting impact on my heart. It taught me that even in the most unexpected moments, in the quiet corners of our lives, magic can happen, and connections can be forged in the unlikeliest of places.

ENCOUNTER #7 The Truck Stop Encounter

The rumble of my truck echoed against the tall Oregon trees, creating a melody I'd grown used to. The mountains, painted with the orange and pink hues of the setting sun, watched over me like ancient guardians. I, Jake, had been driving these roads for over a decade and a half. Though the scenes were familiar, every drive felt like a new journey.

The dashboard blinked, warning me of the long hours I had been behind the wheel. I could feel the weight of the day pressing on my eyelids, urging me to find a spot to rest. Thoughts of my wife, Emma, and our two children flooded my mind. This job took me far from them, but it was for them that I worked these long hours.

Ahead, the familiar sign of a truck stop came into view. It was a well-known resting point for me, a small oasis amidst the vast landscape of Oregon. I looked forward to the simple comforts it offered, a break from the road's monotony.

Once I parked my truck, I took a deep breath, cherishing the cold bite of the Oregon air. This was always my spot, on the farthest end of the stop, away from the crowd. There was something about this corner that felt more private, more personal, like a secret space just for me.

Stretching my limbs, I decided to grab some food. My stomach growled in agreement. As I walked into the truck stop, the delicious aroma of grilled food hit me. Familiar faces greeted me, fellow drivers I'd come to know over the years.

Inside, the place buzzed with conversations. There were stories of the road, shared laughs over traffic snarls, and exchanged notes on the best routes. Amidst the chatter, I collected my meal, eager to return to the sanctuary of my truck.

The comfort of my sleeper cab welcomed me. This was my mobile home, where I unwound and escaped the world outside. Tonight, like many nights, I'd planned to watch a movie while enjoying my meal. The soft glow of the screen lit up the space as an old western film began to play.

But something felt off tonight. Out of the corner of my eye, I spotted a fleeting shadow outside. At first, I brushed it off, thinking it might be another trucker. I tried focusing back on my movie, but the uneasiness lingered.

Then, the shadow passed by again. This time, it was longer and more deliberate. A cold shiver ran down my spine. Muting the film, I tried to get a better look outside, wondering if someone might be playing tricks on me.

Curiosity pushed me to peek through the window. What I saw next was something I'd never imagined. A tall, hulking creature stood at the edge of the truck stop. The dim lights faintly illuminated its form, revealing a figure unlike any man or animal I'd seen.

It moved with an unusual grace, its long arms swaying with every step. The creature seemed to be covered in a thick, shaggy fur. Though its face was hidden in the shadows, its powerful build was undeniable. The way it moved, the aura around it, was wild and untamed.

I instinctively ducked, trying to process what I'd seen. My heart raced. Questions filled my mind. What was that creature? Was it dangerous? I decided to watch, hidden from its view, as the creature moved closer to the woods, eventually disappearing into the thickets.

The night grew colder and darker after the creature's departure. I locked the doors of my truck, hoping for some semblance of security. The thought of sleep seemed impossible, with my mind replaying the eerie sighting over and over.

The minutes felt like hours. The usual night sounds of the truck stop seemed more pronounced, each one making me jump. I tried distracting myself, playing soft music in the background, but the image of the creature loomed in my mind.

Deciding that I might feel better after talking to someone, I thought of heading inside the truck stop once morning came. Perhaps someone else had seen it too, or maybe they'd heard stories. As dawn approached, with a sense of apprehension, I prepared myself for another day on the road.

The morning light gently seeped through the windows, signaling a new day. My body felt stiff from the tension and the lack of sleep. Trying to shake off the remnants of the eerie night, I stepped out of my truck, feeling the cool morning air embrace me.

The truck stop was slowly coming to life. Other truckers were also preparing to get back on the road, while some were heading inside for a morning coffee or breakfast. The normalcy of the scene was in stark contrast to the unsettling encounter from the night before.

Walking into the truck stop, the familiar aroma of brewing coffee hit my nostrils. I stood in line, hoping the caffeine could help clear my mind and battle the fatigue. But more than that, I had questions, and I hoped someone inside could provide answers.

Holding my steaming cup, I hesitated for a moment, then mustered up the courage to ask the young clerk behind the counter. "Have you ever heard of anyone seeing... anything strange around here at night?" My voice quivered slightly, not knowing what reaction to expect.

The young woman looked up, her expression thoughtful for a moment, and then broke into a playful smile. "Strange? Oh, every day!" she chuckled. "Almost every trucker that comes through here is strange in their own unique way." She gave a wink, thinking I was referring to the eccentric personalities of some drivers.

It was clear she had no inkling of what I was truly asking about. I forced a smile, deciding not to press further. Maybe it was best to leave some mysteries unsolved. With my coffee in hand, I thanked her and headed out, the weight of the unknown still pressing on my shoulders.

Back in my truck, I settled into my seat, preparing for another long drive. As I started the engine, the rhythmic hum comforted me, a reminder of the countless miles I'd traveled and the many stories I'd collected along the way.

The Oregon landscape began to unfurl around me. With each passing mile, the truck stop and the mysterious encounter receded into the distance. Yet, my mind kept wandering back, trying to make sense of what I'd seen. Was it possible that legends like Bigfoot were rooted in truth?

The hours rolled on, but my thoughts were consumed by the creature. Its powerful form, the eerie way it moved, and its disappearance into the woods all played on a loop in my mind. Every shadow, every movement in my peripheral vision, made me wonder if it was lurking nearby.

Thoughts of my wife and kids brought some comfort. Their smiles, their laughter, the memories we shared. The distance from them always felt vast during my drives, but the events of the previous night made me yearn for their presence even more.

I wondered whether I should share the encounter with Emma. She was always my confidante, my anchor. But the thought of causing her unnecessary worry made me hesitate. Would she believe me, or would she think it was just the product of an overtired mind?

The roads stretched endlessly ahead. Trucks passed by, each with its own story, its own journey. Maybe some of the drivers had their own unexplained encounters, their own mysteries they carried with them. The road was full of secrets, and perhaps I had just stumbled upon one of its biggest.

The sun began its descent, casting a golden hue over the landscape. The day was coming to an end, and with it, my drive. My home, with its familiar comforts and the embrace of my loved ones, awaited.

The closer I got to home, the more the idea of sharing my encounter weighed on me. I wanted to protect Emma and the kids from the dangers and mysteries of the road. Sharing my story would only add to their worries.

Finally, as the familiar landmarks of my neighborhood came into view, I made a decision. This mystery, this encounter, would remain my secret. A personal chapter in the long book of my life on the road. As I parked my truck and stepped out, I took one last look at the horizon, wondering if the creature was out there, continuing its own enigmatic journey.

ENCOUNTER #8 The Mistaken Identity Encounter

It was a regular morning in our small Oregon town of Ashland. The sun peeked through the trees, casting long shadows on the roads. Birds chirped their familiar melodies, greeting the day. I sipped on my black coffee, looking at the small stain on my uniform that my wife always teased me about.

My day started slowly, just like most others. Parking disputes, kids speeding; it was the usual chatter over the police radio. As the morning progressed, I began to lose myself in thoughts of home, of how my daughter was doing in school, and if I'd get some time off next month.

But then, an unusual call came in, breaking the monotony of the day. An elderly gentleman, Robert, reported a shadowy figure lurking near his house, possibly a homeless person. It seemed strange for our town, a place where everyone knew everyone.

As I drove to Robert's house, the memories of my previous interactions with him came rushing back. I remembered his kind eyes, his soft-spoken nature, and the way he would always offer me a glass of lemonade during our community meetings. His house, sitting right at the edge of town, had always seemed so peaceful.

Robert's wife, Susan, was waiting for me at the porch, her face strained with worry. Her shaky voice detailed how she saw the shadow by their shed when she came home from work. Robert added his account, saying he too had seen this mysterious figure.

I could sense their fear, and it was contagious. The thought of someone intruding on this quiet couple's life didn't sit well with me. The mystery thickened as both mentioned signs of someone, or something, staying in the woods behind their home.

The woods had always been a place of solace for me. As a child, I'd spend hours wandering its paths, letting my imagination run wild. But today, as I ventured into it, the woods felt different, more ominous.

Each rustle of the leaves, each snapping twig made me more alert. The more I searched, the more I began to see evidence of a makeshift camp. There was a clear trail, flattened grass, and discarded wrappers that led me deeper into the woods.

My mind raced. Who could be living here? And why? As I moved further in, a chill ran down my spine. There was a sense of being watched, but every time I turned around, there was nothing.

My search was coming up empty. The dense forest swallowed all evidence of the mysterious intruder. It was quiet, too quiet, making me feel even more on edge. I needed to reassure Robert and Susan but didn't know what to tell them.

As I made my way back to their house, the sun began to dip below the horizon. The shadows grew longer, and the chirping of the birds was replaced by the haunting calls of the owls. I relayed my findings to Robert and Susan, advising them to stay vigilant and call if they saw anything amiss.

The drive back to the station was filled with a nagging unease. I couldn't shake the feeling that I was missing something crucial. The unknown, the idea of something lurking just out of sight, was a thought I couldn't escape.

The next couple of days were uneventful. Routine calls filled my days, pushing the mysterious figure to the back of my mind. But the peace was shattered two nights later. Robert's panicked voice crackled through the radio. The shadow had returned.

With my heart pounding in my chest, I sped to their house. The night was unusually dark, the moon hiding behind a thick blanket of clouds. Robert, looking even more distressed than before, pointed to the spot where he'd seen the shadow.

Taking a deep breath, I moved towards the area. Each step felt heavier than the last. With my flashlight cutting through the inky darkness, I began my search. The night sounds seemed to amplify, making the tension palpable. The mysterious intruder was here, and I was determined to uncover the truth.

The backyard, bathed in eerie moonlight, stretched out before me, bordered by dense trees. I could barely make out the silhouette of the shed, where the mysterious figure had been seen before. With every rustle of the leaves, my anticipation grew, wondering if I'd finally confront the intruder.

My flashlight's beam scanned the yard, revealing nothing unusual. It's funny how even a simple tool like a flashlight can feel like a lifeline when you're plunged into the unknown. I continued my search, trying to cover every inch of the yard, hoping to find any clue or sign.

But it was the sudden sound from the bushes that grabbed my attention. As I pointed my flashlight in the direction of the noise, the light caught the eyes of a creature, reflecting a deep, unsettling red. I stood frozen, trying to make sense of what I was seeing.

The creature's face, illuminated by my flashlight, was something out of a storybook. A massive brow ridge, a flat nose, and dark, matted hair covering most of its features. But what struck me most was the surprise in its eyes. It was as if it hadn't expected to be seen.

For a moment, time seemed to stand still. Every detail of the creature, its towering stature, its muscular frame, was etched into my memory. My hand instinctively moved to my pistol, but the creature, realizing it was spotted, darted away with remarkable speed.

All I could do was watch as the figure vanished into the depths of the woods. The reality of what I'd seen was beginning to sink in, and a mixture of fear and awe washed over me. I wasn't dealing with a mere human intruder. This was something entirely different.

Slowly, I made my way back to Robert, who was anxiously waiting by his house. His eyes searched mine, looking for answers. "I think you have something more than a homeless person back there," I muttered, my voice barely above a whisper.

Robert's face went pale, sensing the gravity of the situation. He tried to probe further, asking about what I had witnessed. But, unable to process my own feelings, let alone put them into words, I only warned him to be cautious and vigilant.

The drive back to the station that night was one of the longest I've ever experienced. The weight of the unknown pressed down on me, and the image of the creature's face haunted every shadow, every turn.

Days turned into weeks, and life in Ashland resumed its peaceful rhythm. Yet, the memory of that night lingered in the back of my mind. Every time I drove past Robert's home, a chill ran down my spine, reminding me of the creature's haunting gaze.

I grappled with whether to share my encounter with my fellow officers. The fear of being ridiculed, of not being believed, held me back. After all, who would believe in the existence of such a creature in our quiet town?

One evening, as I patrolled the same area near Robert's house, I couldn't help but pull over and gaze into the woods. The questions swirled in my mind: What was that creature? Where did it come from? And most importantly, where had it gone?

Despite the unanswered questions, the sightings stopped. Robert and Susan reported no further disturbances, and the town's chatter about a mysterious intruder gradually faded. But for me, the mystery remained alive.

Each time I passed by that area, an unsettling feeling would take over. The unknown, the idea of a world beyond what we see and understand, was both intriguing and frightening. The woods, which once held fond memories of childhood adventures, now held a deeper, more profound mystery.

Every now and then, when the night is particularly dark and the wind rustles the trees, I find myself thinking about the creature. Though our paths crossed only once, the impact was lasting. And as I continue my duties, patrolling the quiet streets of Ashland, I can't help but wonder what other mysteries lie hidden, just beyond our sight.

ENCOUNTER #9 The Delivery Driver Encounter

The early morning sun cast a pale golden hue over Astoria, Oregon. Birds sang their cheerful songs, and a cool breeze rustled the leaves. I always loved mornings like this. They made waking up early for my UPS job a bit easier.

Starting as a loader at UPS was hard work. Heavy packages, long hours, and the hum of trucks became my daily routine. But over the years, I'd climbed the ladder. Now, I was a driver. No boss over my shoulder and the open road ahead; I cherished every bit of it.

The town of Astoria had its secrets. Secrets that were whispered in quiet corners and discussed in hushed tones. While I knew most of the streets and buildings like the back of my hand, there was always that hint of mystery, a feeling that something unexpected was just around the corner.

Morning routines are comforting, a kind of anchor to the day. Mine always began with a hot cup of coffee, its aroma wrapping around me like a cozy blanket. Then, there was Amy, my girlfriend. Her smile was the second dose of warmth I needed to kickstart the day.

Today was special, and I had a surprise planned for her. Three years of togetherness, and it felt like yesterday that we met. I made a mental note to pick up a bouquet of her favorite flowers later in the day.

Setting out on my route, the familiarity of the town greeted me. The local bakery, Mrs. Hansen's delightful treats, the chatter of the townsfolk; all of it painted a serene picture. But today, the air felt different, charged with an unusual energy.

It was mid-morning when I approached the retail store. I was lost in thought, mentally arranging my packages for quick delivery. Suddenly, a strange shadow at the edge of my vision grabbed my attention.

I turned my head, trying to focus on what caught my eye. And there it was, a creature, tall and imposing, standing at a distance. It wasn't human, but neither did it resemble any animal I'd ever seen. It moved with purpose, its eyes darting around, taking in its surroundings.

A chill ran down my spine. The field behind the store was mostly empty, with a few shrubs and trees lining its edges. I had never seen anything unusual there before. Today, however, the vast open space held a secret, one that would change everything.

Regaining my composure, I drove slowly to the store's loading dock. My mind raced, trying to make sense of what I had seen. Was it just my imagination playing tricks? Or had I truly seen something out of the ordinary?

As I prepared to unload, the back door of the store creaked open. A young employee, probably fresh out of high school, peeked out. He looked at me, his expression changing from anticipation to concern. "You look like you've seen a ghost," he remarked.

I hesitated, then decided to share. "I saw something in the field. Not sure what it was." He shrugged, mentioning the recent bear sightings in the area. But deep inside, a voice told me that what I'd seen was no ordinary bear.

The day wore on, and I continued my rounds, yet my mind was elsewhere. Every shadow, every rustle in the trees, made me jumpy. The town's everyday charm now held a layer of mystery that was hard to shake off.

Late afternoon, as I drove past the forest's edge, the dense canopy seemed to whisper tales of old, stories of creatures and legends. I wondered if what I had seen was known to others. Had anyone else experienced what I had?

As the sun set, casting long, eerie shadows across the town, I felt an urgency to share my experience. I decided to confide in Amy. She was my rock, my sounding board, and I knew she would listen without judgment. With the bouquet of flowers clutched tightly in one hand and a heart full of anxiety, I headed home, eager yet fearful of unburdening my day's experience.

The soft glow of the porch light welcomed me as I pulled up to our home. The house, with its white picket fence and warm wooden exteriors, had always been a place of comfort. I could hear the muffled sounds of Amy inside, probably preparing dinner.

With the bouquet behind my back, I entered. Amy's face lit up in surprise when she saw the flowers, but her joy was short-lived. Noticing my troubled expression, her smile wavered. "What happened?" she asked, her voice thick with concern.

Taking a deep breath, I began recounting my morning's experience. Each word, every description, was met with wide-eyed attention from Amy. When I finished, she sat quietly for a moment, processing what I had shared. "Could it be...the bear everyone's been talking about lately?" she finally ventured.

I leaned back on the couch, the weight of the day's events pressing down on me. The image of the creature was imprinted on my mind. "It was no bear, Amy," I whispered, my voice steady but filled with the weight of conviction. "Its eyes, the way it moved...it was something else."

Amy walked over to the window, peering out into the darkening night. "You know, there have always been stories," she began, her voice soft, "Legends of creatures that dwell in the deep woods of Oregon. My grandma used to tell me tales."

I looked at her, intrigued. "What tales?" I urged. She hesitated, then sighed. "Stories of Bigfoot, the elusive giant. Some say it's just a myth, while others swear they've encountered it. I always thought it was just to scare the kids, but now..."

Our dinner lay forgotten on the table. The cozy room was filled with an electrifying tension. We both dived deep into our memories, recollecting every piece of local lore we had ever heard.

"The way you described it, Ethan, it does sound like the legends," Amy admitted. "But it's been years since anyone talked about a real sighting. Most people nowadays dismiss it as mere folklore."

"I can't dismiss what I saw," I replied, frustration evident in my tone. The evening was slipping away, and the house was filled with a blend of fear, curiosity, and the need to understand. The known boundaries of reality seemed to blur, making room for the mysterious.

As night deepened, we decided to do some research. Pulling out old books and scouring the internet, we were on the hunt for any recent sightings or information that matched my experience.

To our astonishment, there were more accounts than we'd imagined. Some were from decades ago, while others were more recent. Photographs, sketches, and vivid first-hand accounts painted a picture that was hard to ignore.

Despite the overwhelming evidence, a part of me still grappled with doubt. But another part, the part that had seen that creature, knew that there was more to this world than meets the eye. And that sometimes, myths are born from a kernel of truth.

Amy and I talked late into the night, discussing every possibility. At some point, fatigue took over, and we found ourselves curled up on the couch, drifting into a restless sleep filled with dreams of giant creatures and ancient woods.

Morning came with the soft chirping of birds. The previous day's events felt distant, almost like a dream. But the books scattered across the floor and the open pages on the laptop were proof of our nocturnal quest for answers.

We decided not to tell anyone for now. The town was small, and rumors spread like wildfire. But in the quiet moments, when the wind rustled through the trees and shadows played tricks on the mind, we would exchange knowing glances. We had peered into the mysterious, and our world had changed forever.

ENCOUNTER #10 The Bedtime Snack Encounter

Life hadn't been kind to me in recent years. Once upon a time, there was Peter and me, so deeply in love that we thought nothing could separate us. But life had its own mysterious ways, and the fairy tale love story ended abruptly, leaving me to fend for two young souls.

My children, Jamie and Ellie, were my heart and soul. Jamie was the elder of the two, always inquisitive, often lost in his own world, asking countless questions about everything under the sun. Ellie was my ray of sunshine, her giggles filling our home with warmth.

After Peter left, I decided that a fresh start was needed. With the little savings I had, I rented a small house in Oregon, hoping that the dense forests and serene environment would provide the healing we all needed. The house, though tiny, felt like home.

Every evening had a routine. Once dinner was done, and the kids had finished their homework, it was time for some relaxation. I would turn on the TV to play "Mystical Adventures," a show about magical realms that Jamie and Ellie absolutely adored.

The soothing tunes from the show gave me some moments of calm. I would sit on our old couch, watching my children's faces light up in wonder as the characters embarked on their adventures. The stresses of the day seemed to melt away in those moments.

Tonight, as the familiar theme song played in the background, I felt a pang of nostalgia. It reminded me of simpler times, before responsibilities weighed heavy. Yet, amidst the challenges, there was always a glimmer of happiness watching my kids engrossed in their favorite show.

Hoping to make the night even more special, I quietly sneaked into the kitchen. My plan was simple: surprise Jamie and Ellie with a bowl of goldfish crackers. As I reached for the jar, a memory flashed before me.

Jamie, in his typical mischievous style, had once tried to keep a real goldfish inside this very jar. The memory brought a soft chuckle. I could still hear Ellie's giggle and Jamie's plea to keep the fish as a pet.

With two bowls filled to the brim, I headed back to the living room. The cartoon's voices echoed softly, and the dim room was lit by the TV's glow. It was the perfect ending to a long day, or so I thought.

Walking back to the living room, something unusual caught my eye. From the window's corner, I saw a fleeting shadow. At first, I dismissed it, thinking it might be a neighbor or a stray cat. But curiosity gnawed at me.

Placing the bowls on the coffee table, I tiptoed to the window, trying not to alarm the kids. As I peered outside, my heart skipped a beat. There, across the street, was a figure unlike anything I'd ever seen.

It ambled along the ditch, its movements stealthy yet awkward. The street was silent, and all I could hear was the soft hum of the TV and the pounding in my chest. I blinked, trying to make sense of what I was seeing.

The moon hung high in the night sky, casting a silvery glow that illuminated the creature. It stood tall, maybe eight feet or more. Its physique was rugged, covered in thick, dark fur that shimmered under the moonlight.

Its face was what captivated me the most. It was eerily human-like, with deep-set eyes that seemed to reflect a world of emotions. The eyes glistened, and for a moment, I felt an inexplicable connection.

The creature continued its march, attempting to stay concealed. But as if sensing my gaze, it suddenly stopped, our eyes locked in a silent confrontation. A chill ran down my spine, a mix of fear and wonder.

The connection, as intense as it was, lasted only a brief second. But in that fleeting moment, so much was communicated: curiosity, understanding, and perhaps a mutual respect for each other's existence. It was as if two worlds, so vastly different, collided for just an instant.

The creature's eyes bore into mine, and I could sense a weariness in them, almost as if it too had lived a life fraught with challenges and loneliness. Then, without warning, it turned, its massive frame beginning to move away, its strides cautious yet assertive.

My heart raced as I wrestled with the decision to rush out and follow it, or stay put, nestled in the safety of my home. As it disappeared into the cloak of the dark, I found myself standing there, utterly transfixed, the bowls of goldfish crackers forgotten.

It took a few minutes before I could tear myself away from the window. My mind was ablaze with questions, and my heart pounded with adrenaline. Was that really Bigfoot, the mysterious creature of the Oregon woods, or just a figment of my overtired imagination?

I questioned my sanity. After all, the struggles of being a single mother, the loneliness and the responsibilities, could have taken a toll on me. Could my mind have concocted this strange, almost mystical encounter as a form of escapism?

Yet, the image was vivid, the emotions real. My legs, feeling strangely numb, carried me back to the couch. My eyes met with Jamie and Ellie's curious gazes, their faces illuminated by the flickering TV light, completely oblivious to the strange occurrence just beyond our door.

Ellie's gentle voice broke through my daze. "Mommy, what were you looking at?" Her innocent eyes searched mine, and I quickly masked the shock with a reassuring smile. "Just the beautiful moon, sweetheart," I replied, forcing normalcy into my voice.

I nestled myself between them, my arms enveloping them with all the love I felt. I kissed their heads, inhaled their sweet scent, and felt a strange sort of peace settle over me. Whatever I had witnessed did not matter; I had my children, and they were safe.

As the final credits of their show rolled, Jamie and Ellie, now calmed by their snack and show, snuggled closer. The world outside, with all its mysteries and possible threats, seemed distant and irrelevant in comparison to the cozy bubble we had inside.

Once the kids were tucked into bed, their breaths steady and soft in the quiet room, I found myself sitting alone in the dark, the image of the creature's eyes imprinted in my mind. The house was silent, save for the distant calls of nocturnal animals from the forest beyond.

I thought about its fur, deep brown with tinges of gray, and those eyes that seemed to carry centuries of stories. What was its story? Was it, too, a creature burdened with its own sorrows, wandering through the darkness, searching for some sort of meaning?

And then a realization washed over me. The creature, despite its strangeness, had its own place in this world. It belonged to the dark, mysterious forests of Oregon, just as I had found my place in this tiny rented home with my two beautiful children.

Days turned into weeks and slowly, the incident became a distant memory. But every night, as I gazed out of the window at the moon, I would think of it, somewhere out there in the vast wilderness, under the same glowing orb.

I never spoke of the incident to anyone, not even to Jamie and Ellie. It became my secret, a mystery that I would carry with me. But it was more than just an encounter; it was a reminder of the world's vastness and the countless mysteries it held.

In the quiet of the night, I would sometimes hear distant howls and rustles from the dark forest. And I would sit there, a silent observer, understanding that just like us, the creature had its own life, its own struggles, and its own stories to tell, under the same moonlit sky.

ENCOUNTER #11 The Road Repair Encounter

The early morning sun peeked through the thick clouds, casting a warm, golden light over the winding Oregon hill. Our team's truck rumbled to a stop next to a mangled guardrail. I stepped out, taking a deep breath of the fresh mountain air. The guardrail, twisted and bent out of shape, told a silent tale of a terrible crash.

My teammates, Mark, Jim, Dave, and the others, gathered around, taking in the scene. We'd been through dozens of repairs that summer, but this was a bad one. Mark, ever the theorist, mumbled, "Probably some late-night party-goer who had one too many." Dave, shaking his head, countered, "Or someone who can't resist texting while driving. Can't count how many times I've seen it."

From the state of the wreckage, we could tell the driver must've been going pretty fast. I touched the cold metal, wondering what really went through the driver's mind in those final moments. The forest, dense and full of shadows even during the day, stood as a silent witness.

The day's work began with the usual energy. Machines roared to life, their hum filling the air. We set out the cones and got to work, each of us knowing our roles perfectly. It felt good being part of a team that functioned like a well-oiled machine.

While we worked, the banter never stopped. From Dave's new ridiculous haircut to Jim's failed fishing trip last weekend, nothing was off-limits. With every joke and laugh, the morning seemed to fly by. The sound of our laughter mixed with the mechanical rhythm of our work.

By noon, we'd made good progress. I paused, wiping the sweat from my brow, looking at the dense woods across the road. There was something oddly captivating about them. It felt as though they held secrets known only to the trees and creatures within.

After a hearty lunch, my bladder reminded me of its presence. "Hey, taking a short break, guys!" I called out. I made my way across the road, towards the woods. The trees, tall and majestic, seemed to reach for the sky. Their leaves whispered secrets, rustling in the soft wind.

As I found a secluded spot, I felt the weight of the forest around me. Every chirp, every rustle felt amplified. It was a world away from the bustling road. With every step deeper, the world outside seemed more distant, the forest enveloping me in its serene embrace.

I was about to head back when a subtle rustle stopped me. It wasn't the rustling of leaves or the scurrying of a small animal. It was different. Curiosity piqued, I tried to pinpoint the source, my senses on high alert.

My eyes scanned the thick underbrush, searching for any sign of movement. There! About 40 yards away, something stirred. A large shadow, obscured by dense foliage, yet there was no mistaking it. My heart raced, every beat echoing loudly in my ears.

For what felt like an eternity, I stood frozen, eyes locked on that spot. I could make out a face - large, expressive eyes, and a broad nose. It was covered in coarse, matted fur, yet it wasn't any animal I recognized. The creature and I held a silent standoff, neither moving, just observing.

Suddenly, a truck's horn blared from the road, breaking the trance. I blinked, and the creature vanished. The forest, once again, became just a mass of trees and shadows. But I knew what I'd seen, and I couldn't shake off the feeling.

The teasing and laughter of the crew greeted me as I stepped out of the woods. I was still reeling from my encounter, the image of the creature fresh in my mind. "Took you long enough! Were you setting up camp in there?" Jim joked, noticing my dazed look.

I hesitated for a moment, then took a deep breath. "Jim," I whispered, "I saw something. In the woods." His eyebrows shot up, a smirk forming on his lips. "Oh, really? What, a squirrel? Maybe a rabbit?" I shook my head, my voice barely above a whisper, "No. It was... It was big. Like a Bigfoot or something."

Jim burst into laughter, clapping me on the back. "Billy's seeing monsters now! Maybe you should lay off those sandwiches," he teased. But as the crew laughed and the jokes flew, I couldn't shake off the feeling that the woods held more mysteries than we knew.

As the afternoon wore on, the ribbing continued. Mark chimed in with, "Maybe Bigfoot was just looking for some company, Billy!" The laughter was infectious, and even I found myself chuckling, though my mind kept wandering back to the mysterious figure. Dave, always the storyteller, started narrating an exaggerated tale of my encounter, complete with dramatic pauses and hand gestures.

Though I tried to focus on the task at hand, the dense trees across the road beckoned. Every rustle, every shadow seemed to whisper of the enigma I'd faced. The more I tried to dismiss it as a trick of the light or my imagination, the more I felt its presence. The forest, so beautiful and serene, now held a hint of the unknown.

While the crew worked diligently, Jim kept glancing my way, a sly grin on his face. He'd occasionally make big, exaggerated looks towards the forest, mocking fear, only to burst into laughter. And as much as I wanted to shrug it off, I couldn't help but continuously glance back at the woods, hoping for another glimpse.

The sun began its descent, casting long shadows that danced with the breeze. The mangled guardrail now stood straight, a testament to our hard work. But even as we packed our equipment, the forest's allure was undeniable. The crew, sensing my distraction, rallied around for one last round of teasing.

"Hey, Billy," Dave called out, feigning seriousness, "maybe we should set up a camera here. Get a reality show going – 'Bigfoot and the Repair Crew!'" The crew erupted in laughter, and even I had to admit, the thought was amusing. Jim added with a wink, "And if we don't find Bigfoot, at least we'll catch Billy's mysterious forest adventures!"

Despite the fun and laughter, a small part of me wondered if there was truth in jest. Could the creature I had seen be the same one that had possibly startled the driver, causing the crash? The pieces of the puzzle seemed to fit, but without evidence, it was just a wild theory.

We finally packed up, the last rays of the sun painting the sky a brilliant hue of oranges and pinks. The forest, bathed in twilight, looked serene, almost magical. But for me, it was a reminder of the unexplained, a mystery that I might never solve. The crew's spirits were high, the day's work a success, and the evening promising relaxation.

As we loaded into the trucks, Mark shouted, "Last one in is Bigfoot's dinner!" The challenge was met with laughter and a playful race to the vehicles. Yet, as we settled in, the joking subsided, replaced by the tired satisfaction of a job well done.

The engines roared to life, the sound echoing in the stillness. And as we drove away, the winding road and the looming forest seemed to merge into one, the trees standing as silent sentinels, guardians of their secrets.

The road stretched on, the journey back filled with light banter and recollections of the day. Dave turned on the radio, filling the truck with soft melodies. Every song, every note seemed to blend with the evening, creating a harmonious symphony.

Yet, my thoughts kept drifting back. The creature's face, so vivid in my memory, seemed to taunt me. Every rustling leaf, every moving shadow on the roadside, made me jump, half expecting to see it again. "You okay there, Billy?" Jim's voice, filled with genuine concern, broke my reverie. I nodded, forcing a smile, "Yeah, just a long day."

But as the miles passed, a thought took root. The damaged guardrail, the mysterious creature, the crash - were they all connected? Could the driver have seen the same creature I did, resulting in the accident? The idea, far-fetched as it seemed, was oddly compelling.

As we neared our base, the lights of the town greeted us, a comforting beacon against the encroaching darkness. The forest, with all its mysteries, was now behind us, yet its shadow loomed large in my mind.

Jim, sensing my unease, tried to lighten the mood, "You know, Billy, if you're that curious, we could always camp out there one night. See if your friend shows up!" I chuckled, "Maybe we should. But only if you're on night watch!" We both laughed, the tension easing.

But as the evening wore on and the trucks were parked, the crew dispersing to their homes, I couldn't shake off the day's events. Standing there, looking back at the now distant hills, I wondered if some mysteries were meant to remain unsolved. And maybe, just maybe, the forest and its inhabitant would continue to be one of them.

ENCOUNTER #12 The Trout Encounter

The early morning sun streamed through the curtains of Joe's bedroom, casting a warm glow across the room. Today was going to be special. Not only because Joe, my best buddy, was spending the whole day with me, but because we had planned a fishing adventure. Our parents had been friends since forever, which meant Joe and I practically grew up together, sharing countless adventures.

We started the day as we often did, challenging each other to a video game. With controllers in hand, we tried our luck, failing more than succeeding, but always laughing. The game's graphics danced on the screen, and the sound effects filled the room, but after a while, the digital world just couldn't compare to the call of the great outdoors.

"I think it's time for some real action," Joe whispered, his eyes glinting with excitement. I nodded in agreement. We'd talked about fishing for a while now. Today seemed like the perfect day to bring our fishing dreams to life. So, we decided to leave the virtual world behind and embrace the real adventure awaiting us.

We packed our gear quickly: fishing poles, bait, and a few sandwiches for the journey. The air outside was fresh, carrying a hint of the upcoming rain, as we set out on our bikes. Our village, a picturesque countryside, was dotted with familiar landmarks and houses that held memories of our shared childhood.

As we rode, we passed Mrs. Benson's place. Her old dog, Max, as always, barked cheerily, wagging his tail. It was like a ritual; every time we passed, he'd give us this joyful greeting. Further down the lane, old man Jacob was in his garden, lost in the world of his blooming flowers. We exchanged waves and smiles, the familiarity comforting.

The path to our secret fishing spot was one we'd taken countless times before. But today, something felt different. An unusual mist enveloped the surroundings, giving the landscape an almost magical appearance. The promise of mystery and adventure was in the air, making our hearts race with anticipation.

Reaching the riverbank, the world seemed to stand still for a moment. The thick mist made the water appear as if it was a vast, endless void. Every now and then, a fish would leap, breaking the water's surface, and the soft splash would echo in the quiet. The day was perfect for fishing, and the atmosphere felt almost dreamy.

We found a spot, settled down, and cast our lines. The gentle rhythm of the river, combined with the distant sounds of nature, was hypnotic. We talked in hushed tones, sharing stories and joking about who would catch the biggest fish. It was one of those times when everything just felt right, and the world outside seemed distant.

Time seemed to fly, and soon enough, we had already caught three trouts each. Proud of our catch, we contemplated whether to continue or head back. But the strange aura of the day made us curious to see what else it had in store. So, we decided to stay a bit longer, not knowing that this decision would change the course of our day.

Joe was the first to spot it. His gaze fixed on something in the distance, his face pale. "Tim," he whispered, "Do you see that?" I followed his gaze, trying to peer through the mist. There, far off on the same side of the river, stood a shadowy figure. It looked like a person, but something about it felt... off.

The mist played tricks on our eyes, making it hard to focus. But as the minutes ticked by, and a breeze momentarily pushed the mist aside, we got a clearer view. The figure was huge, much taller than any man we'd ever seen. Its dark silhouette contrasted sharply against the pale backdrop, making it look even more eerie.

We exchanged glances, our fishing forgotten. Our minds raced, trying to make sense of what we were seeing. Was it someone from the village? Or a stranger who'd wandered into our secret spot? The air grew colder, and the mist thickened, shrouding the mysterious figure once more.

Our eyes remained fixed on the spot where the figure had stood. Slowly, the mist began to lighten again, revealing the creature in its entirety. Its dark brown fur covered its body, shimmering with the moisture in the air. The creature's long, muscular arms reached into the river as if searching for something.

Before we could even process what we were witnessing, the creature made its move. In a swift, fluid motion, it plunged its hand into the river, pulling out a large, wriggling trout. The creature held the fish, inspecting it for a moment, its deep-set eyes reflecting a strange intelligence.

The moment felt surreal. Our minds struggled to comprehend the reality of what we were witnessing. Was this a dream? Or were we really seeing a creature of legend right before our eyes? Before we could decide, the creature turned and disappeared into the thick woods, leaving us in stunned silence.

The echo of the creature's departure reverberated in our ears. Joe and I sat, motionless, as the reality of what had just transpired settled in. The atmosphere around us had shifted from one of quiet serenity to palpable tension. The gentle ripples in the river and the distant chirping of the birds now felt eerie and foreboding.

"I... I think we just saw Bigfoot," Joe stammered, his voice barely above a whisper. I tried to respond, but the words got caught in my throat. My mind raced with a flurry of thoughts. Could it have been just a very tall man? Or maybe it was an optical illusion caused by the mist? But deep down, I knew that neither explanation felt right.

We slowly began to pack up our fishing gear, our earlier enthusiasm replaced by a nervous energy. Every rustle in the trees, every splash in the water, made us jump. The dense fog that had earlier felt magical now felt like a shroud, masking dangers unknown.

As we made our way back to our bikes, our earlier chatter was replaced by heavy silence. Our shared experience had bound us in a new way, creating an unspoken understanding. Every now and then, one of us would glance back towards the spot where we had seen the creature, half expecting to see it emerge from the fog.

The ride back home was a blur. The landmarks and houses that had earlier felt comforting now seemed to watch us with suspicious eyes. The mist had begun to lift, replaced by a light drizzle that tapped on our helmets and jackets. But even the rain couldn't wash away the shock and amazement from our faces.

"Tim," Joe said, breaking the silence, "We've got to talk about what we saw." I nodded, knowing that this was a story we couldn't keep to ourselves. But would anyone believe two young boys who claimed to have seen a legendary creature on a foggy afternoon?

Upon reaching my house, we rushed to find my mom. We found her in the kitchen, preparing dinner. Without waiting for a greeting, we spilled out our story, words tumbling over each other in our excitement and fear. The tale of the mysterious giant creature, its deep-set eyes, and its incredible fishing skills poured out of us like a torrent.

My mom listened patiently, a smile playing on her lips. "You boys and your adventures," she said, chuckling. "It must have been a very tall fisherman. This mist can make things look strange." But Joe and I exchanged glances, knowing that what we'd seen was no ordinary man.

Dinner that night was a quiet affair. The usual banter was replaced by reflective silence. Joe and I were lost in our thoughts, replaying the day's events over and over. The creature's image was etched into our minds, and we knew that this was a memory that would stay with us forever.

That night, as we lay in our sleeping bags, the darkness outside was punctuated by the soft glow of a night lamp. The events of the day weighed heavy on our minds, and sleep seemed like a distant possibility. "Do you think it'll come back?" Joe whispered, his voice echoing my own thoughts.

"I don't know," I replied, my voice shaky. "But we need to find some proof. We can't let this story die with us." We talked into the night, brainstorming ways to prove our encounter was real. We spoke of setting up cameras, of revisiting the spot, of searching for footprints.

But as the hours ticked by, our fear and anxiety gave way to exhaustion. Slowly, the weight of our eyelids became too much to bear. As sleep claimed us, our minds were filled with dreams of misty rivers, giant creatures, and mysteries waiting to be uncovered.

The morning sun seemed to shine a little brighter, chasing away the remnants of the previous day's fog and fear. But the memory of our encounter was as vivid as ever. Over breakfast, we recounted our story to my dad, hoping for a more believing audience.

He listened intently, his eyebrows furrowing in thought. "It's possible you saw something unusual," he said. "But the woods are full of mysteries. It's best not to dwell on them." Joe and I nodded, but we knew that forgetting wasn't an option. Our curiosity was piqued, and we were determined to find answers.

The day passed in a blur, but the memory of our encounter was a constant companion. Every rustle, every shadow seemed to hint at the presence of the unknown. As the sun set, painting the sky in hues of orange and pink, Joe and I made a silent pact. We would return to the river, not just as fishermen, but as explorers, determined to uncover the secrets it held.

ENCOUNTER #13 Orchard Encounter

The sun began to rise over our family's cherry farm in Oregon, casting a golden hue on the vast orchard. Every morning, I took a jog along the cherry tree-lined paths, feeling the soft grass beneath my feet. The brisk air filled my lungs, and with every stride, memories of my grandparents' tales of the farm danced in my mind.

After the jog, I would sit down to breakfast, always at the old wooden table that had been in our family for generations. The smell of Mom's cooking wafted from the kitchen, promising a hearty meal. Today, she was preparing a quiche, its aroma mixing perfectly with the faint scent of ripening cherries.

As I bit into a slice, my thoughts wandered to the stories my grandparents used to tell. Tales of strange occurrences on the farm, whispers among the trees, and shadows that moved just out of sight. I would always laugh them off, but sometimes, on quiet mornings like this, I'd wonder.

Over breakfast, Mom and Dad discussed their day's plan. They needed to make a trip to town for some farm supplies. As I listened, my gaze wandered outside, where our farm workers were already busy inspecting the trees and tending to the ripe cherries.

Dad began to tell a story, one he had heard from his grandfather. It was about a mysterious figure seen wandering the orchard many years ago. He described it as a mere shadow, almost blending into the night. It would appear and then vanish, leaving no trace behind.

My younger siblings, Ben and Emma, listened with wide-eyed fascination, hanging on to every word. But I had heard this story countless times and just smiled, taking another bite of my quiche. As Dad finished, the room filled with soft chuckles and murmurs about old family legends.

With breakfast over, I decided to lend a hand in the orchard. The sun was now high in the sky, its rays filtering through the leaves of the cherry trees. As I walked, I noticed Miguel, a loyal worker who had been with our family for years, looking intently at something in the distance.

Curiosity piqued, I approached him. Miguel seemed a bit startled and mentioned he thought he saw something. A figure, not quite clear, moving between the trees. He quickly dismissed it as a trick of the light. Still, the story Dad had just told echoed in my mind, making me a bit uneasy.

I shook off the feeling and continued my tasks. The orchard was always full of sounds - birds chirping, leaves rustling, and distant conversations. But today, something felt different. The air felt a bit heavier, and an eerie silence seemed to hang over certain parts of the orchard.

As the day wore on, Mom and Dad prepared to head to town. I offered to watch over things while they were away. Just as they were about to leave, a mysterious howl echoed from beyond the hill. It was unlike any sound I had ever heard.

We all paused, looking around to identify its source. The howl seemed to vibrate in the very air around us, its haunting notes lingering for what felt like minutes. Unsure of what it was, we tried to brush it off, thinking maybe it was just a distant wolf or coyote.

However, the howl left an unsettling feeling in its wake. Mom and Dad exchanged worried glances but said nothing. They left, but the echo of that sound stayed with me, amplifying the mysterious atmosphere that seemed to have enveloped our farm.

Later in the afternoon, I spotted Miguel near the irrigation system. He was trying to fix a damaged hose, frustration evident on his face. Wanting to help, I started walking toward him. As I approached, I could sense something was off. Miguel kept glancing towards a particular row of cherry trees, his brow furrowed.

Following his gaze, I squinted to see if there was anything unusual. For a brief moment, I thought I saw a tall, shadowy figure standing near one of the trees. But when I blinked, it was gone. The feeling of unease returned, now stronger than ever.

Miguel and I locked eyes. We both knew we had seen something, but neither of us wanted to acknowledge it. Trying to break the tension, Miguel joked about the heat playing tricks on our eyes. But the truth was, both of us felt the weight of the orchard's mysteries pressing down on us, reminding us that some stories might be more than just tales.

The rest of the afternoon was a blur. I tried focusing on my tasks, but the events of the day played continuously in my mind. My thoughts kept drifting back to the shadowy figure by the cherry trees. Every rustle of the leaves, every unexpected sound made me jumpy.

Miguel suddenly approached me, looking more disturbed than before. He hesitated, then began to describe his encounter in detail. The creature he saw had dark, matted fur and was much taller than a regular person. It had been plucking cherries and when Miguel had shouted, it looked straight at him. The eyes, a mesmerizing shade of amber, seemed to see right through him.

The way he described the creature, it sounded nothing like any animal native to our area. Remembering the old stories

Dad shared, a chilling thought entered my mind. What if the legends were true? What if there really was something or someone living in our orchard, hidden away from the world?

Not wanting to jump to conclusions, I decided to see the spot Miguel was talking about. We hopped on the family's old ATV, and he directed me towards the row of cherry trees where he had the encounter. The journey there was silent, save for the soft hum of the ATV's engine and the thoughts racing through my mind.

When we reached the spot, I noticed the ground was slightly disturbed. And there it was: a footprint. It was huge, much larger than a human's, and had a unique pattern. The realization hit me hard. Miguel wasn't exaggerating. He had indeed seen something.

We sat there, side by side, neither of us speaking for a while. The silence of the orchard seemed louder than ever. A gentle wind rustled the cherry leaves, but it did little to ease the tension. There was no denying it now; we weren't alone in the orchard.

We headed back to the main house, the weight of our discovery hanging between us. As the ATV trundled along the path, memories of the stories I once laughed at filled my mind. Those tales no longer seemed like mere bedtime stories but warnings handed down through generations.

When we arrived at the house, we decided to sit on the porch and process everything. The evening sun cast long shadows, and the chirping of crickets began to fill the air. With glasses of iced tea in our hands, we weighed the pros and cons of sharing our discovery.

After a long discussion, I suggested that maybe it was best to keep this to ourselves for now. The farm was not just our home, but our legacy. Stories like these, true or not, could spook others and affect our livelihood. Miguel agreed, and we decided to guard this secret together.

The night settled in, bringing with it a mix of serenity and uncertainty. Ben and Emma were playing in the yard, their innocent laughter providing a brief distraction from the day's events. Mom was inside, humming a tune as she prepared dinner, unaware of the mysteries unfolding outside.

Sitting on the porch, I went over the farm's records, trying to distract myself. But every rustling leaf, every unknown sound seemed magnified, making concentration impossible. The orchard's mystery loomed over me, and even the familiar sights and sounds of our farm now felt alien.

As the evening wore on, a sense of acceptance began to replace my initial shock. The farm had been in our family for generations, and maybe this creature, whatever it was, had always been a part of it. Instead of fear, I started feeling a strange connection, a tie to the land and its hidden stories.

The hours flew by, and soon, it was time to retire for the night. As I made my way to my room, the day's events played in my mind. The farm, with its vast expanse of cherry trees, had always been my sanctuary, but today, it had shown me a side I never knew existed.

I sat by my window, looking out at the moonlit orchard. The silver light bathed the trees, making their shadows dance. Every now and then, a breeze would carry the sweet scent of cherries. The farm was alive in its own mysterious way, and I felt a renewed sense of respect for it.

With a sigh, I lay down, trying to get some sleep. But the image of the footprint and the amber-eyed creature haunted my dreams. While the creature remained elusive, one thing was clear: our farm was not just a simple orchard. It was a land of legacy, stories, and mysteries waiting to be unraveled.

ENCOUNTER #14 The Road Crossing Encounter

The early morning sun peeked through the blinds, casting a golden hue across the room. I stretched and blinked, welcoming the familiar sounds of birds outside. My wife, Rachel, already awake, moved about with her morning rituals. The scent of fresh coffee wafted through the air, reminding me of the challenges the day ahead would bring.

I leaned over, giving Rachel a gentle kiss, feeling the warmth of her skin against mine. "Busy night?" I asked, knowing she'd just returned from her overnight shift at the hospital. She nodded, her eyes a mixture of exhaustion and contentment. Our conversations were brief in these wee hours, but they were our special moments, shared in the quiet of the morning.

Our two little ones, still deep in sleep, lay bundled up in their blankets. I tiptoed into their room, watching them breathe, lost in dreams. My heart swelled with pride and love. It's amazing how such tiny beings can fill a room with so much joy and purpose.

I had always cherished the bond I shared with my parents. Growing up, our house was always filled with laughter, stories, and adventure. Dad would take me out on weekend trips, teaching me the ways of the wild. Meanwhile, Mom would share tales from her childhood, speaking of legends and mysterious creatures that roamed the forests of the Pacific Northwest.

With every story she told, my imagination would run wild. I'd envision a world filled with magical creatures, hidden treasures, and untold adventures waiting to be discovered. My mother's voice, filled with warmth and excitement, would transport me to those magical realms, making me yearn for my own adventures someday.

I couldn't help but feel grateful for the memories and lessons my parents instilled in me. Their stories not only fueled my imagination but also taught me the value of family, love, and staying connected to one's roots.

The kids had a routine at Grandma's, one that they looked forward to each day. My mother, though older now, never let age dampen her spirits. Today, I could picture her laying out colorful papers, glues, and paints, ready to help the kids create a masterpiece.

In my mind's eye, I could see them sitting under the huge oak tree in her backyard, cutting, pasting, and chatting away. My mother's voice would be filled with patience and encouragement as she guided their little hands, helping them bring their imaginations to life on paper.

I knew the kids would later come home, their faces glowing with pride, eager to show me their creations. Those scrapbooks weren't just pages filled with pictures and colors; they were memories, testimonies of the precious time they spent with Grandma.

I climbed into my car, adjusting the rearview mirror. The drive to pick up the kids was a ritual I cherished. The route was scenic, surrounded by tall pine trees, their branches swaying to the gentle breeze. A soft tune played on the radio, adding to the serenity of the journey.

As I drove, my mind wandered. I found myself reminiscing about the past, a time when life was simpler. Childhood memories flooded in, making me smile. The fishing trip with Dad, the first time I set up a tent, and those chilly nights around the campfire – all these memories came rushing back.

The soft hum of the car engine, combined with my memories, lulled me into a calm state. I occasionally glanced at the rearview mirror, noticing the familiar road behind, its turns and bends marking my journey back to the two most important people in my life.

The trees along the road seemed to whisper tales of the past. Every curve and corner had a story to tell. As a child, I remembered running through these woods, feeling the thrill of adventure with every step. The forest was my playground, a place where I felt free and alive.

I recalled that sunny afternoon when I proudly showed off the fish I had caught to my parents. Dad's eyes sparkled with pride, and Mom's warm hug made me feel like the hero of the day. Those moments were simple, yet they held a special place in my heart.

Lost in these thoughts, I hardly noticed the car's gentle rhythm lulling the kids to sleep. Their little heads bobbed side to side with the car's movement. I smiled, realizing that, like me, they too would have their stories to tell about these woods someday.

The road ahead was clear, the sun casting long shadows that danced with the swaying trees. The calmness was suddenly broken by a swift, unusual movement. From the swampy region to my right, something large and dark emerged, making its way across the road. My grip tightened on the wheel, my senses on high alert.

This wasn't just any animal; it was massive, covered in thick, matted brown fur. But what caught my attention the most were its eyes, deep-set and intensely focused, revealing a mysterious intelligence. As it moved, I could sense its power, its presence commanding my full attention.

As quickly as it appeared, the creature darted towards the woods on the left. The world seemed to move in slow motion as I tried to process what I had just witnessed. My heart raced, the weight of the moment pressing down on me. It was a creature of legend, one that my mother had spoken of in her tales.

My gaze followed the creature as it effortlessly navigated the rugged terrain. With each stride, its powerful muscles flexed, showcasing its raw strength. There was a grace to its movement, a primal elegance that was both mesmerizing and intimidating.

As it reached the dense woods, I caught a final glimpse of its form. Its broad shoulders, sturdy legs, and the way it moved hinted at a life spent surviving in the wild, evading predators and humans alike. The forest swallowed it up, its form blending seamlessly with the trees and underbrush.

A chill ran down my spine. My mother's tales never described the creature in such vivid detail. I felt a mix of awe and fear, my mind racing, trying to make sense of what I had just witnessed. Was this the mysterious Bigfoot of legends?

Regaining my composure, I instinctively looked in the rearview mirror, half-expecting to see wide-eyed children staring back, their faces a reflection of my own disbelief. Instead, I was met with the peaceful faces of my sleeping kids, their breaths steady, undisturbed by the recent events.

Relief washed over me. I wasn't sure how I would have explained such an encounter to them. Children have a way of sensing things, of picking up on the unspoken. I hoped that the serene expressions on their faces meant they had missed the whole thing.

Shaking my head, I continued my drive, the events playing in my mind like a movie reel. The mysterious creature, the woods, the stories – everything seemed to be connected in some inexplicable way.

As I pulled into the driveway, the familiar sight of our home brought a sense of comfort. Rachel was up, her figure silhouetted against the window, probably getting ready for another grueling night shift. The sight of her anchored me back to reality, reminding me of the life we'd built together.

Stepping out of the car, I took a deep breath, the fresh air filling my lungs. I helped the kids out, their sleepy faces scrunching up at the sudden brightness. They ran into Rachel's open arms, her laughter echoing in the still afternoon air.

Rachel's eyes met mine, her gaze searching, probing. "Everything okay?" she asked, her voice filled with concern. I hesitated for a moment, the weight of the encounter still fresh. But seeing my family, safe and happy, I replied, "Just a long day," keeping the mystery to myself.

Inside, the house was filled with warmth and familiarity. The kids settled into their routine, their giggles and chatter filling the rooms. I found myself lost in thought, the image of the creature replaying in my mind. The intensity of its gaze, the power of its stride, it was all too real to be a figment of my imagination.

As Rachel left for work, I held her a little tighter, a little longer. She looked at me, her eyes filled with questions, but she didn't press further. Some secrets, I realized, are meant to be kept. As the day drew to a close, I sat by the window, watching the sun dip below the horizon, its orange glow casting long shadows, much like the secrets I now held within me.

ENCOUNTER #15 The Teacher's Encounter

The gentle rays of morning sun washed over my bedroom, pulling me out of a deep slumber. Today was the day I'd been waiting for, our 5th-grade class trip to Silver Falls State Park. The air held a crispness that hinted at the promise of adventure, and I couldn't help but let my mind drift to my childhood.

Every memory was laced with the scent of pine and the whisper of wind rustling through trees. My father, an outdoorsman to the core, had imparted his love of nature to me. Those days, when he'd teach me about the beauty hidden in every leaf and the stories told by the mountains, were the most treasured moments of my life.

Now, as a teacher, I wanted to pass on the wonderment I felt during those days to my students. I hoped that this field trip would be a memory they'd hold onto, just as I clung to memories of my father and our time in the wilderness.

As I reached the school, the palpable excitement of the students was infectious. The gleaming yellow school bus waited in the driveway, and Mr. Mason, our gentle-natured driver, greeted each student with his characteristic warm smile.

Then there were our chaperones, Mrs. Griffin and Mr. Diaz. Both parents were as enthusiastic about the wilderness as I was. Mrs. Griffin's laugh was hearty, echoing through the schoolyard as she chatted with the kids. Mr. Diaz was quieter, always carrying a book about local flora and fauna, ready to share a fun fact.

We were a motley crew, each bringing our unique energy, but all united in our anticipation for the day ahead. As the bus rumbled to life and we made our way to Silver Falls, I watched the world outside and wondered about the day's mysteries.

Silver Falls was a masterpiece of nature. The sound of water cascading down the rocks resonated deep within, invoking a sense of serenity. The kids' eyes widened as they beheld the breathtaking sight for the first time, and I saw reflections of my younger self in their awe-filled expressions.

I began sharing stories and knowledge about the park, each fact more intriguing than the last. The moss-covered stones, the peculiar chirping of the birds, and the unique flowers that seemed to nod in agreement with every word I said. The atmosphere was alive with curiosity and wonder.

The dense forest surrounding the falls was a tapestry of green, dotted with bursts of color from wildflowers. A soft, cool mist from the waterfall hung in the air, making the world feel like a dream. But as much as I tried to focus on teaching, there was an unshakable feeling that we weren't alone in this wilderness.

Lunchtime arrived, and we found a perfect spot right by the falls. The students gleefully unpacked their sandwiches and snacks, chattering away. Tommy, a boy with disheveled hair and ever-curious eyes, was particularly engrossed in observing a butterfly.

Mrs. Griffin pulled out a guitar, filling the air with soft melodies that harmonized with the surroundings. Mr. Diaz showcased his collection of leaves, making the kids guess the names of the trees they belonged to. As laughter and music swirled around, the mysterious feeling I had earlier seemed to fade, but only momentarily.

Time flew by, and soon it was time to pack up and head back. We checked to ensure we hadn't left any trash behind. The environment was, after all, a treasure we had to protect. As we left the area, Tommy's butterfly had led him slightly astray, his backpack forgotten amidst the lush grass.

The path back was lined with tall trees, their canopies forming a green tunnel. But the journey was interrupted by Tommy's sudden realization. His face drained of color as he stammered out that he'd left his backpack behind.

I could see the worry clouding his bright eyes, so I assured him, promising to retrieve his lost item. Instructing Mrs. Griffin and Mr. Diaz to lead the group back to the bus, I began my journey back to our lunch spot. With each step, the atmosphere grew denser, the earlier feeling of being watched returning stronger than before.

The forest was quieter now, save for the distant murmur of the falls. My senses heightened, every rustle, every whisper of the wind felt like a secret being shared. A mix of anticipation and uncertainty gripped me, but my resolve to retrieve Tommy's backpack drove me forward into the mystery that awaited.

The familiar spot by the waterfall came into view, but something felt off. My heart raced as I spotted a figure, unlike anything I'd seen before, hunched over Tommy's backpack. It was massive, standing on two legs, its body covered in a thick coat of dark fur.

I took a moment to gather my thoughts, trying to comprehend what stood before me. Its face, however, was its most striking feature. Deep-set brown eyes, filled with a blend of curiosity and caution, looked over the backpack. The creature's broad nose twitched, perhaps picking up a scent, and its mouth hinted at a gentle disposition despite its colossal form.

Frozen in place, a whirlwind of emotions surged through me. Fear, fascination, and an overwhelming realization that I was witnessing something truly extraordinary. This wasn't just any forest dweller; it felt like I was gazing upon a legend.

Suddenly, our tranquil standoff was broken as a twig snapped beneath my foot. The creature's gaze shifted from the backpack directly to me, our eyes locking in a moment of shared surprise. It seemed as bewildered by my presence as I was of its.

Neither of us moved for what felt like an eternity. The waterfall's roar faded into the background, replaced by the intense heartbeat echoing in my ears. In that fleeting moment, I felt an unspoken understanding between us, a mutual respect born from the surprise of our unexpected meeting.

As quickly as it had appeared, the creature turned, releasing its grip on the backpack. With agility surprising for its size, it disappeared into the depths of the forest, leaving behind a world forever changed for me. I was left alone once more, the weight of what I had just witnessed pressing heavily upon me.

Shaking off the shock, I approached the forgotten backpack. There, clear as day, was a large muddy handprint smeared across its fabric. It was undeniable evidence of my encounter, yet I knew it would be hard for anyone to believe.

My return journey to the bus was a hurried one, each shadow in the forest, every distant noise making me jump. The forest had transformed from a familiar sanctuary to a place filled with enigmas and unanswered questions.

Finally reaching the bus, I was met with anxious faces. Tommy rushed forward, relief evident as he clutched his returned backpack. However, he didn't seem to notice the muddy handprint, too engrossed in the joy of having his belongings back.

The ride back to the school was filled with the students' animated chatter, their discussions of the day's adventures filling the air. Their innocent excitement provided a stark contrast to the turmoil of thoughts swirling in my mind.

Mrs. Griffin shared stories of the kids' antics while I had been away, while Mr. Diaz sat engrossed in his nature book, occasionally sharing interesting tidbits. The normalcy of their actions was a balm to my frayed nerves.

I leaned back in my seat, the weight of my secret pressing down on me. The forest, the waterfall, and that mysterious creature seemed like fragments from a dream. Yet, the muddy handprint on Tommy's backpack was a tangible reminder of the day's unbelievable events.

The next morning in the classroom, the atmosphere buzzed with the students' renewed energy. Eager to channel their enthusiasm, I assigned them a task: to pen down their most memorable experience from the field trip.

As I watched them scribble away, I couldn't help but let my mind wander. If only I could share my own extraordinary tale, but the world wasn't ready for such a story. It was a secret that needed protection, both for the sake of the mysterious creature and the magic of the unknown.

The bell's chime snapped me back to reality, my students' stories in hand, each a testament to their unique perspectives. Yet, hidden within my heart was a tale that would remain untold, a secret memory of an encounter in the heart of Silver Falls State Park.

ENCOUNTER #16 The Dishwasher's Encounter

I remember the day like it was yesterday, although it felt much longer than just a couple of months. Every morning, I would reluctantly wake up, quickly munch on whatever breakfast I could find, and head straight to Mama Jo's Diner. I had been working there since I was fifteen, washing dishes and trying my best not to lose myself in the never-ending stream of dirty plates and glasses.

The job wasn't fun, not at all. In fact, I had started browsing online job listings in the mornings, imagining a life away from the constant noise of the kitchen and the splattering of water. On this particular day, after browsing through countless offers, I sighed deeply. I thought, 'Almost any job would be better than this. Even just sweeping floors.'

It wasn't just the work, but the people. The other staff, especially Tom, the lead cook, seemed to have it out for me. It felt like every small mistake I made became a big issue.

Tom's sharp words and quick temper made me dread going to work more than anything else.

The day progressed as usual. The lunch crowd started pouring in, and the dishes piled up. One after another, plates with leftover gravy, half-eaten burgers, and smudged silverware landed in my sink. The water, mixed with tiny bits of food, kept splashing onto me, staining my clothes and making me feel sticky and grimy.

Before heading to work that day, I had made a small detour. I stopped by the local store and picked up a case of pop. Thinking of the cold drink kept me going through the scorching afternoon. Parking my old, hand-me-down car near the diner, I left the windows down, hoping the breeze would offer some respite from the summer heat.

It was a simple, unassuming vehicle, but it was mine, a symbol of my freedom. Every time I looked at it, I dreamt of the places I could go, the adventures waiting for me, and maybe, just maybe, a life beyond this town and its suffocating routine.

7:00 PM on the dot, my break time. It was the only time in the day when I could truly be myself, even if it was just for a short while. I made my way to my car, the anticipation of a cold drink and some quiet time pushing my tired legs.

Reaching into the back seat, I grabbed a soda and turned on the car radio. The calming tunes filled the car, making me momentarily forget my worries. I took a moment to just breathe, to take in the evening, and to dream of better days.

My gaze wandered, and soon I found myself staring into the dense woods adjoining the diner's parking lot. It was peaceful, with the setting sun casting long, mysterious shadows. A slight rustling caught my attention. Probably a raccoon, I thought. But then, an overwhelming and unfamiliar stench began to fill the air.

Intrigued, I decided to investigate the source of the smell. Maybe it was a discarded food item or a forgotten trash bag. But deep down, a voice told me it was something else. I stepped out of the car, the cold pop can still in my hand, and slowly approached the forest's edge.

The darkness within seemed to pull me in, the sense of mystery growing with every step. My heart raced as the trees grew denser, the world outside fading away. Suddenly, a moonbeam pierced the canopy, revealing something I had never seen or imagined.

A towering figure stood a few feet away. Its body was covered in a mix of black and brown fur, but it was its face that captured my undivided attention. Deep, piercing eyes stared back at me, reflecting a strange intelligence. The wide, flat nose and thin-lipped mouth seemed almost human, but the sheer size and presence of the creature were anything but.

Time seemed to slow as the creature and I stood there, locked in a silent standoff. My mind raced, trying to comprehend what I was seeing. Was it a bear? A man in a costume? But neither explanation fit the creature in front of me.

I could hear the creature's breath, a deep and rhythmic sound that hinted at its size and strength. The stench became more pronounced, a mix of damp earth and something wild. I felt a chill run down my spine, realizing just how close I was to something truly unknown.

The pop can slipped from my fingers, the sound of it hitting the ground shattering the silence. The creature took a step back, its gaze never leaving mine, before slowly retreating into the darkness of the woods. I was left standing there, trying to process what had just happened, my world forever changed.

Regaining my senses, I looked down at the spilled soda, its contents forming a small puddle by my feet. The cool evening breeze reminded me of the world outside the woods, and I turned back towards my car. The events from the last few minutes replayed in my mind, making me doubt if it was real or just a product of my imagination.

But the overpowering stench still lingered, a testament to the creature's presence. My heart raced as I entered my car, feeling an urgent need to put some distance between the woods and myself. The calming tunes from the radio now seemed eerily out of place, and I switched it off, lost in my thoughts.

Reaching the diner, the harsh reality of my job awaited. I could still hear the clinking of dishes and the distant chatter of customers. But the noise now seemed far away, muffled by the overwhelming emotions and questions swirling in my head. Was I ready to go back to the mundane after witnessing something so extraordinary?

Without much thought, I walked straight into the diner, the noise and heat enveloping me once again. My once heavy apron now felt like a shackle, reminding me of the countless hours I had spent washing dishes, all the while dreaming of an escape. The spilled food, the mocking glances, the endless work—it all suddenly seemed insignificant.

Tom, the lead cook, noticed my entrance and sneered, "Back from your break already? Did you daydream long enough?" But his taunts fell on deaf ears. With newfound determination, I made my way to the manager's office.

Placing my dirty apron on the desk, I declared with confidence, "I quit."

The manager, taken aback, looked at me with surprise. "You sure about this?" he asked. I nodded, realizing that after tonight, I was no longer the same person. I needed change, a fresh start, and a life that was truly mine.

The following days were a whirlwind. While the memory of the creature haunted my dreams, my waking hours were filled with job applications and interviews. Mama Jo's Diner and its grimy dishes seemed like a distant memory. Fate, it seemed, was finally on my side.

I landed a job at the local grocery store. The work was simple—bagging groceries and helping customers. But to me, it felt like freedom. The friendly chatter of customers and the smell of fresh produce were a welcome change from the stifling atmosphere of the diner.

The other employees were kind and welcoming, making me feel at home. The weight of the past year started lifting, replaced by a sense of hope and excitement. Each day was a new opportunity, a chance to learn, grow, and, most importantly, be happy.

As days turned into weeks, I settled into my new role. I loved my job and the new friends I had made. Yet, the memory of that evening by the woods lingered, urging me to find answers. I often found myself gazing into the woods as I drove past Mama Jo's, wondering if the creature was real or just a figment of my imagination.

But as much as curiosity tugged at me, I never ventured back into the woods. The creature, whether real or imagined, had changed my life for the better, giving me the push I needed to break free from the diner's clutches. Sharing my encounter with others never crossed my mind, fearing ridicule or disbelief.

Instead, I cherished the memory, keeping it close to my heart. It became my little secret, a mysterious chapter in my life that only I knew about. It was a constant reminder that the world was full of wonders, and sometimes, all we needed was a little nudge to discover them.

As I looked ahead, the future seemed bright. The once monotonous routine had transformed into a journey of discovery and growth. Every morning, I would wake up with a smile, eager to face the day and its challenges.

The grocery store became my second home. My colleagues became my family, supporting and encouraging me at every step. The customers, with their stories and anecdotes, added color to my life, making each day unique and special.

Yet, every time I passed by the woods near Mama Jo's, a sense of wonder and gratitude filled me. Whether it was fate, destiny, or just a chance encounter, that evening had set me on a new path. And as I looked back at the twists and turns of my journey, I realized that sometimes, the most unexpected events could lead to the most beautiful destinations.

ENCOUNTER #17 The Morning Hike Encounter

Every morning was a fresh start, but today felt different. Nestled on the edge of Oregon was the state park that had become my haven. The tall trees, the crisp air, and the scent of pine needles greeted me as the first rays of sunlight pierced through the leaves. As I tied my shoelaces, I felt a mixture of excitement and nervousness. Today wasn't just about my early morning hike; it was also the day of the blind date my sister, Emily, had arranged for me.

Despite being successful in my finance job, my personal life was like a jigsaw puzzle with a missing piece. The long hours at work and the constant stress left me little time for dating, and my heart felt heavy. To manage it all, I took my hikes seriously, using them not only to stay fit but also to escape and find peace. Today, however, with the date looming over me, peace seemed elusive.

The winding path beckoned. With each step, the anxieties of life faded into the background. The familiar chirping of the birds, the rustle of leaves, and the gentle flow of the river nearby eased my mind. The trail had become my confidant, always ready to listen and never judging.

Stretching my muscles, I felt the tension slowly release. A sip of water and I was ready to conquer the trail. For breakfast, I had my usual – a granola bar and some fresh fruit, enough to keep me energized. I took a moment to look around, soaking in the beauty that surrounded me, and feeling grateful for these moments of solitude.

On most days, my hikes were like meditative sessions. But today, thoughts of the impending date with a man I'd never met kept creeping into my mind. I wondered if he'd like me or if we'd have anything in common. Emily had insisted that he was a good match, but I wasn't convinced.

The sun was slowly climbing higher, casting a golden hue on everything. Birds flew overhead, their silhouettes dark against the bright sky. Their carefree nature made me wish I could be one of them, even if just for a day.

One foot in front of the other, I trekked along the path I knew so well. Memories of past hikes flashed before my eyes: some filled with laughter and friends, others with contemplative silence. But every hike had been a journey, both physical and emotional. The steady rhythm of my footsteps became a comforting soundtrack, allowing me to lose myself in my thoughts.

Suddenly, a cool breeze brushed against my face, bringing with it the distinct scent of rain. I looked up, noticing the previously clear sky now dotted with gray clouds. It wasn't forecasted to rain, but nature had its own plans. The woods held many secrets, and even though I had been here countless times, there were always new mysteries waiting to be discovered.

Ahead, the path took a familiar bend. I could almost walk it with my eyes closed. Little did I know that rounding that curve would change everything.

The air grew heavier, charged with a strange energy. As I rounded the bend, my steps faltered. There, right in the middle of the path, stood a creature I had only heard of in legends. Tall and covered in thick fur, it was unlike anything I had ever seen. The very air around it seemed to tremble, filling me with a mix of awe and fear.

We locked eyes, and for a moment, time seemed to stand still. The creature's gaze was deep, holding a mix of curiosity and surprise, as if it hadn't expected anyone to be there. I was rooted to the spot, my mind racing, trying to make sense of the surreal scene unfolding before me.

Then, as if waking from a dream, the forest came alive again. Birds chirped, and the leaves rustled, but the creature and I remained locked in a silent standoff. A myriad of questions rushed through my mind. Was it as surprised to see me as I was to see it? Was it dangerous? What should I do?

Suddenly, the creature let out a howl that sent shivers down my spine. The sound was so raw and primal; it echoed through the woods, silencing everything in its path. My heart raced, every instinct screaming at me to run. Yet, my feet refused to move, as if glued to the ground.

The creature's intense gaze never wavered, but I could sense a change in its demeanor. It seemed as startled by its own howl as I was. Slowly, realization dawned upon me: this creature, as mighty as it appeared, was as vulnerable and taken aback as I was.

However, survival instincts kicked in, and before I could process the situation further, I turned and ran. Each stride was powered by adrenaline, my mind singularly focused on getting away. The howl still echoed in my ears, a chilling reminder of the unknown mysteries the forest held.

As I sprinted away, the trees blurred into a green tunnel, each footfall echoing my rising heartbeat. Every rustling leaf or breaking twig jolted my nerves, making me question if the creature was chasing me. The familiar landmarks of the trail seemed foreign, and I yearned to be out in the open, far from the mystery that lurked behind me.

Finally, the edge of the forest came into view, and my car sat there, gleaming under the morning sun. Never had I been so relieved to see it. Once inside, I locked the doors and took deep breaths, attempting to calm my racing heart. I glanced back towards the trail, half-expecting to see the creature emerge, but all remained still.

Questions swirled in my mind. What was that creature? Why was it there? And why, of all days, did our paths cross today? But the most nagging thought of all was whether anyone would believe my story. I started the car, driving away from the forest that held my secret, a forest that had lost its innocence in my eyes.

Walking into the office, the usual buzz of phones ringing and colleagues chatting felt distant. My desk, littered with paperwork and the blinking computer screen, seemed unimportant. Every time I closed my eyes, the image of the creature flashed before me. It was hard to focus on numbers and sales pitches when my mind was consumed by the morning's events.

By lunchtime, I realized I couldn't go through with the date Emily had set up. The thought of making small talk while my mind was in turmoil felt insurmountable. Taking out my phone, I sent her a quick text, canceling our plans. Her response was swift and laden with disappointment. I wished I could explain, but how could I convey the weight of my experience in a simple text?

The rest of the day dragged on, with me mechanically going through the motions. The conversations with clients, the meetings, and even the casual coffee breaks felt like a blur. My heart wasn't in it, and my mind was a million miles away.

Sunday couldn't come fast enough. I had agreed to meet Emily for lunch, and the weight of the secret I was carrying felt heavy. As I saw her across the cafe, her familiar smile greeting me, a rush of emotions flooded in. Emily had always been my confidant, and I knew I could trust her with anything.

With a deep breath, I began recounting the events of that fateful hike. Describing the creature in detail, from its thick fur to its penetrating gaze, I tried to paint a vivid picture. Emily's eyes widened with every word, her disbelief evident, but she listened without interrupting.

By the time I finished, the cafe around us seemed to have quieted, as if even the universe was waiting for her response. She took a moment, processing the enormity of what I had just shared. Then, gently, she reached out and took my hand, her touch grounding me.

"I believe you," Emily whispered, her eyes sincere. Relief washed over me. But then she added, "But not everyone will. Stories like these... they can change how people see you." I nodded, understanding her concerns. The world was often unkind to those with tales that strayed from the ordinary.

Emily, ever the protective sister, suggested we keep my encounter a secret. She feared for my reputation, for the whispers and the judgment that might follow. And as much as I wanted to share my story with the world, I knew she was right.

We made a pact, right there in the cafe, sealing my story between us. It became our shared secret, a bond that deepened our already close relationship. As we parted ways, I felt a mixture of gratitude and sadness, knowing the forest's secret was safe, but also wondering if it was right to hide the truth.

The following days were a whirlwind of emotions. At times, I'd catch myself staring into the distance, the image of the creature vivid in my mind. But having shared my story with Emily, the weight I felt had lightened. The secret that we now held brought us even closer, and I found solace in her understanding and support.

My hikes continued, but now with a heightened sense of awareness. Each rustling leaf or distant howl made me wonder if the creature was near. Yet, despite the fear, a part of me yearned to see it again, to seek answers to the myriad of questions that haunted me.

The forest, with all its mysteries, remained my sanctuary. But now, every hike was tinged with anticipation and caution. The path ahead was uncertain, but I knew one thing for sure - I was no longer alone in my journey.

ENCOUNTER #18 The Lost Dog Encounter

The morning sun poured into my room, making the wooden floor warm beneath my feet. I stretched, feeling the pleasant tingle of anticipation for the day ahead. Today was just like any summer day, yet there was a special memory that always made me smile. It was the day I had chosen Brutus from the Humane Society.

The memory was still so clear. The Humane Society, with its sterile smell and echoes of excited barking, was overwhelming at first. My parents had been hesitant, watching me cautiously, probably expecting my enthusiasm to wane. But then, in a cage towards the back, a playful mix of German Shepherd and Husky had caught my attention.

Brutus, as I later named him, wagged his tail and barked, not aggressively, but as if to say, "Choose me! Choose me!" That connection, the instantaneous bond, was what convinced my parents. As we left with Brutus by my side, I couldn't contain my happiness, promising them I'd be the best dog owner ever.

Our house was located far from the town's hustle and bustle, surrounded by dense woods. The chirping of the birds and the soft breeze rustling the trees provided a peaceful background soundtrack to our daily lives. My parents worked in town, leaving me with hours of alone time, which was why they thought Brutus would be good company.

There was a downside, though. Despite his gentle nature, Brutus had a wild streak. He loved running, and if not on a leash, he'd chase after anything that moved. My parents had warned me multiple times about his adventurous spirit, and I'd always promised to be careful.

That day, the sky was a clear blue, and the sun shone brilliantly. Planning to make the most of it, I decided to play some basketball. As I laced up my sneakers, Brutus watched, his tail wagging, sensing an adventure was about to begin.

The basketball felt cool in my hands as I dribbled it down the driveway. The repetitive bounce echoed around, occasionally interrupted by Brutus's playful barks. Suddenly, a squirrel darted across, and before I could react, Brutus was off, chasing it with wild abandon into the woods.

Panic surged through me. The forest was vast and filled with secrets that even I, having grown up here, hadn't uncovered. I bolted after him, the echoes of his barking guiding me deeper and deeper. With every step, the woods grew denser, and the familiar paths seemed to twist into unfamiliar patterns.

The game of basketball was long forgotten. All that mattered now was finding Brutus. His barking was my North Star, leading me further. But then, just as suddenly as it started, the barking stopped, replaced by an eerie silence that sent chills down my spine.

The woods around me seemed to change. The trees stood taller, their shadows deeper and the birds' chirping grew distant. My heart raced, each thud echoing in my ears. The sunlight that had previously pierced through the canopy now seemed muted, casting a dim light that made everything appear hazy.

I called out for Brutus, my voice quivering. The quiet was overwhelming, like a thick blanket muffling all sounds. Every rustle, every distant birdcall made me jump. I felt a cold sensation at the back of my neck, as if someone or something was watching me.

Determined to find my dog, I mustered the courage to continue, telling myself that this was just a part of the forest I hadn't explored before. But deep down, a nagging feeling hinted that I had ventured into a part of the woods that held mysteries no one knew.

Time seemed to blur as I wandered, with no sign of Brutus. The trees around me felt ancient, like guardians of the forest's secrets. As I trudged on, a faint mist began to rise from the ground, swirling around my feet and obscuring the path ahead.

Suddenly, up ahead, I saw a dark, massive figure. It was standing still, an imposing silhouette against the dense foliage. My first thought was that it was a bear, but as I squinted, trying to make sense of what I was seeing, it became evident that this was no ordinary creature.

Cradled in its arms was Brutus, seemingly unharmed but looking scared. The creature, covered in thick fur with a face that exuded a gentle intelligence, locked eyes with me. It was the mythical creature spoken of in hushed tones and campfire stories – a Bigfoot. And right now, it held my dog in its arms.

For a moment, everything seemed to stand still. The forest was silent except for my own labored breathing. Brutus, my playful and energetic companion, was held in the arms of this legendary creature. The tales of Bigfoot always painted it as a mysterious and often intimidating figure, but the creature before me seemed different.

The Bigfoot's eyes were deep and soulful, holding a wisdom that seemed timeless. It looked at me, and then at Brutus, as if trying to communicate something. I took a cautious step forward, every fiber of my being urging me to reclaim my pet.

Brutus, for his part, appeared frightened but not hurt. There was a recognition in his eyes too, as if he knew he had wandered into a domain not meant for him. His tail gave a small wag, but he remained still in Bigfoot's gentle grip.

The dense trees around us seemed to lean in, witnesses to this unusual meeting. The Bigfoot, still locking eyes with me, shifted its stance and slowly extended Brutus towards me. There wasn't a hint of aggression, rather an unspoken understanding that the dog belonged with me.

Taking a deep breath, I stepped closer, reaching out to hold Brutus. As I took him into my arms, a wave of relief washed over me, the weight of my earlier panic lifting. I whispered words of comfort to Brutus, feeling his heart racing against my chest.

The Bigfoot took a step back, nodding slightly. The gesture felt almost human. Before I could say or do anything more, it emitted a low, soft grunt, turned, and began walking away, disappearing into the mist and trees as if it had never been there.

Holding Brutus tightly, I tried to process what had just happened. The encounter felt surreal, like a dream. I had heard tales of Bigfoot sightings in Oregon, but they were often brushed off as exaggerations or plain fabrications. Yet, I had just faced the legend itself.

The journey back home seemed easier. The once ominous woods now felt like a protective cloak, guiding me back. The mysterious haze lifted, replaced by dappled sunlight filtering through the trees. The forest, with all its secrets, had let me in and allowed me to leave unharmed.

As I neared home, I realized I had a monumental decision to make. Do I share my unbelievable encounter with my parents, or do I keep it to myself? Brutus, sensing home, wriggled free and bounded ahead, seemingly unscathed by the day's adventures.

When I finally stepped onto our porch, the sun was beginning its descent, casting a golden hue over everything. The sounds of the forest were replaced by the familiar noises of home – distant laughter, the clinking of dishes, and the hum of a lawnmower from a neighboring property.

Brutus, once again full of energy, chased his tail around the yard, his earlier ordeal forgotten. I watched him, debating internally. My parents would be home soon, and they'd surely notice my disheveled appearance and ask about our day. Would they believe my tale? Or would they think it was just a product of my overactive imagination?

The sound of a car pulling into the driveway snapped me back to reality. Taking a deep breath and straightening my shirt, I decided to play it safe. Some experiences, I reckoned, were too precious, too personal, to be shared and possibly dismissed.

As my parents walked in, they looked at me with a mix of curiosity and relief. "Quite a day you've had, huh?" my dad asked, noticing the scratches and dirt on my clothes. Mom, more observant, looked into my eyes, sensing something deeper had occurred.

I hesitated for a moment, then with a playful grin said, "Brutus and I had an exciting day." The details of the forest, the Bigfoot, and our incredible encounter remained unspoken. It became my secret, a magical memory that would stay with me forever.

That night, as I lay in bed with Brutus snuggled beside me, the sounds of the forest in the distance seemed more profound, more alive. I knew that beyond the trees, in the heart of the woods, mysteries and legends lived, and I had been lucky enough to meet one.

ENCOUNTER #19 The Protected Land Encounter

The morning sun peeked through our apartment window, its rays touching the corners of the room. I stretched out, still feeling the edges of a dream where Teresa and I were standing in front of our very own house. It was going to be a big day, and I had that gut feeling that things would change.

Over breakfast, the aroma of coffee blending with the scent of freshly toasted bread, Teresa and I shared our hopes for the future. We spoke of little feet running through hallways and family gatherings in a spacious backyard. We wanted more than this apartment, and the land we'd recently bought was our first step toward that dream.

Teresa reminded me of her long shift at work, her voice laced with a hint of regret. She wished she could join me on our land, seeing firsthand the start of our shared dream. As I assured her that I'd handle the initial clearing, she gave me a warm, encouraging smile, though her eyes hinted at a mysterious concern.

The journey to the land was always an adventure, driving through winding roads surrounded by dense forests. My thoughts wandered back to the day I discovered this place. It was sheer luck, as I was on my way to see another plot, but fate had other plans.

An old, dusty sign saying "Land for Sale" had caught my attention. I remember thinking how this hidden piece of land had the charm we wanted. Curiosity led me to dial the number, and an old man's voice, coarse yet inviting, offered it for a price too tempting to resist.

Pulling up, I was struck again by its beauty. The trees stood tall, like guardians of an ancient secret. Birds sang, their melodies filling the crisp air. It felt right, this place. Like it was waiting for us, or maybe, it was waiting for something else.

Equipped with my tools, I began marking the trees that needed to go. Every swing of the axe echoed through the forest, making me feel like an intruder in a sacred place. The quiet was almost palpable, only interrupted by the sound of my work and my own heartbeat.

As one tree fell, a swift shadow darted in my peripheral vision. I stopped, trying to convince myself it was just a deer or perhaps a large bird. But there was an unsettling feeling, like being watched from the shadows, which sent shivers down my spine.

Taking a deep breath, I attempted to shake off the unease and continued with my work. The dream of our future home pushed me forward. But that feeling of being watched, it clung to me, growing more intense with each passing minute.

The day, which started bright and promising, was turning into one filled with odd occurrences. First, a rock, seemingly from nowhere, landed with a thud near me. I glanced around, half-expecting to see a mischievous kid hiding behind a tree, but there was nothing.

Trying to brush it off as a fluke, I resumed my work. But the peace was short-lived. A massive log came hurtling towards me. I barely dodged it, my heart pounding loudly in my ears. This wasn't just a coincidence.

My instincts screamed at me to run, but I needed to see. Turning in the direction from which the log had come, I was met with a sight that froze me in place. Not too far away, something large and foreboding was watching me.

This creature was unlike anything I had ever seen. Towering and intimidating, it was covered in thick, matted, dark-brown fur. Its eyes, a penetrating amber, seemed to look right through me, assessing and judging. The face, almost human but not quite, had features that spoke of age and wisdom.

As our eyes locked, a mix of emotions surged within me – fear, awe, and a strange sense of understanding. The creature's broad hands, capable of hurling logs and rocks with ease, now seemed to be in a defensive stance, as if protecting something sacred.

Time felt distorted. A million thoughts raced through my mind. Was this the guardian of the forest? Was I trespassing on sacred ground? Every instinct told me to flee, but my legs wouldn't move. It wasn't until the creature took a step toward me that my survival instincts kicked in, urging me to escape.

Without a second thought, I turned and sprinted toward my truck. The forest, which had seemed so serene and inviting earlier, now felt like a maze of shadows and threats. The ground beneath my feet felt unstable, as if the very earth was urging me to leave.

Reaching the truck, I fumbled with the keys, my hands shaking uncontrollably. I could hear the faint rustling of leaves and the occasional snap of a twig, but I dared not look back. The engine roared to life, and I sped off, leaving behind a cloud of dust and my once-beloved dream.

The drive home was a blur. Trees, roads, and signs all merged into one as my mind tried to process what had just happened. The only thing I was certain of was that I had to get back to Teresa, to the safety of our apartment, and away from that land.

Bursting through our apartment door, I was met with Teresa's surprised face. "You're back early," she said, concern evident in her voice. "I thought you'd be working on the land until late." I simply stared at her, my face drained of color, trying to find the right words.

"That's no longer our land," I finally whispered. Her eyes widened in confusion. "What happened?" she asked, guiding me to the couch. As I recounted the events of the day, she listened intently, her face reflecting a mix of disbelief and concern.

"We can't go back," I concluded, my voice firm. Teresa nodded slowly, her hand squeezing mine. We both sat in silence, trying to grapple with the reality of what had happened and what it meant for our dreams.

The mysterious old man who had sold us the land kept creeping into my thoughts. Desperation to understand drove me to pick up the phone and dial his number. It rang for what felt like an eternity before he answered with a simple, "Yes?"

"Did you know? Did you know what's on that land?" I asked, my voice shaking. There was a long pause, and then he replied, "The land can be sold to anyone. But there's only one true owner." The line went dead before I could respond.

I sat there, the weight of his words sinking in. We had been so excited about the deal, about our future on that land. But now, it was clear. We weren't meant to be there. The land had chosen its guardian, and it wasn't us.

The days following were filled with discussions and decisions. The idea of returning to the land was out of the question, but what to do with it remained. We contemplated selling, but who could we, in good conscience, pass this land and its mysterious inhabitant onto?

In the end, the decision was made easier by the incredibly low price we had originally paid. We chose to keep it, to let it be, untouched and undisturbed. Perhaps, over time, the land and its guardian would forget our intrusion.

We began the search for a new home, one already built, away from mysteries and guardians. The dream of building our own place was replaced with finding a home where we felt safe and where our future family could thrive.

As we settled into our new house in town, far away from the wilderness, life started to regain some normalcy. But the events of that day on our old land were never far from our minds. We found solace in the fact that we were safe, but the allure of the unknown sometimes tugged at our curiosity.

Every so often, when driving around town, a road sign pointing toward our old land would catch my eye. A chill would run down my spine, and I would grip Teresa's hand a bit tighter. We had left that part of our life behind, but the memories remained, serving as a reminder of the mysteries of the world.

We realized that sometimes, dreams change. They evolve based on our experiences and the paths we take. Our dream of building on that land had shifted to creating a safe haven in an existing home. The land and its guardian remained, but in our hearts, we knew who the true owner was.

ENCOUNTER #20 The Rented Camper Encounter

The sun was setting as Todd and I reached our camping spot in Oregon's vast national park. We had been looking forward to this trip for a while. After the busy year we'd had, a weekend of relaxation amidst nature was exactly what we needed. The thought of sharing moments and memories under the starry sky filled me with joy.

Todd had outdone himself this time, surprising me with a rented RV instead of our usual tent setup. The inside was cozy, decorated with soft cushions and a small kitchenette. I could already imagine us snuggling in there, escaping from the world. "No tent hassles this time," Todd winked, watching my delighted expressions.

As night fell, we lit a campfire outside. The orange glow of the flames, the soft crackling of wood, and the serene sound of distant wildlife made everything feel perfect. Our past camping trips flashed before our eyes, reminding us of the fun times and minor mishaps we had shared.

Morning light streamed through the RV windows, rousing me from sleep. I stepped out, taking in a deep breath of the fresh mountain air. Birds were singing, welcoming the new day. But the sight that met my eyes made my heart sink.

Our cooler, which we had carelessly left outside the RV, was now a mess. Half-eaten food, torn wrappers, and spilled drinks littered the ground. "What could've done this?" I wondered aloud. Todd shrugged, looking equally puzzled. We had camped many times before and never faced such a situation.

Deciding to not let the mishap ruin our day, we cleaned up the site. Once everything looked tidy, we headed to the nearby town. It was essential to restock our supplies if we wanted to continue our weekend in the wilderness.

The town was a charming place, with rustic wooden buildings and friendly folks greeting us at every corner. Todd and I wandered into a local diner and enjoyed a hearty breakfast. The pancakes were fluffy, and the maple syrup was the sweetest I'd ever tasted.

While shopping for supplies, we chatted with a few locals who shared stories about the beauty of the national park. We even heard tales about strange happenings in the woods, but we brushed them off as mere campfire tales meant to spook tourists.

By the time we returned to our camping spot, the sun was beginning its descent. But something had changed. At our RV's parking spot was a peculiar stack of rocks, arranged in a way that looked intentional. Neither Todd nor I remembered seeing it when we left.

We stared at the rock formation, puzzled. The formation was intricate, not something the wind or a simple animal could create. The shadows cast by the setting sun made the rocks look even more eerie. I felt a chill run down my spine.

"Do you think someone's playing a prank on us?" I whispered to Todd, trying to make sense of it. Todd didn't answer immediately. He looked around, trying to spot any sign of human activity. "I don't know," he finally said, "but I don't like it."

Despite our unease, we decided to stay. Todd moved the rocks aside while I set up our campsite again. We hoped the night would be uneventful, allowing us to enjoy the tranquility we so desired.

The night came quickly, and with it, a thick blanket of clouds that hinted at impending rain. We could hear distant rumbles of thunder, growing louder with time. Glad to be inside the RV, we felt grateful for the warmth and shelter it provided.

We played a game of cards, trying to distract ourselves from the events of the day. Every so often, a gust of wind would shake the RV, making us jump. "Maybe we should think about buying one of these," I remarked, thinking of how comfortable we were despite the brewing storm outside.

Todd agreed, pointing out how much better it was than being stuck in a tent during a downpour. We laughed, remembering past trips where we had been caught in the rain. But our laughter was short-lived, as an unexpected sound outside the RV caught our attention.

The sound was rhythmic, like someone deliberately knocking on wood. We exchanged glances, both wondering if our ears were playing tricks on us. "Did you hear that?" Todd asked, his voice barely above a whisper. I nodded, unable to find my voice amidst the tension.

Bracing himself, Todd moved towards the window to peek out. The rain was pouring now, making it hard to see anything clearly. The knocking continued, echoing in the otherwise silent night, each knock amplifying our fears. "Maybe it's just a tree branch hitting against something," I suggested, trying to sound logical.

But Todd's face turned pale as he whispered, "I don't think so." His gaze was fixed on something outside the window. I mustered the courage to join him, but nothing could've prepared me for what I saw next. In the distance, barely visible through the thick curtain of rain, was a tall, shadowy figure.

For a moment, time seemed to stand still. The figure, partially hidden by the trees, was unlike anything we had ever seen. It was tall, towering over the surroundings. The rain drenched its furry body, and its eyes glinted with an eerie glow.

Suddenly, lightning illuminated the sky, offering a clearer view. The creature was knocking against a tree, producing the sound we had heard. Its face was humanoid, but its features were exaggerated, giving it a wild appearance. It turned its head, and its piercing gaze met ours.

I could feel my heart racing. Grabbing Todd's arm, I whispered, "We need to leave, now!" Todd nodded, his face ashen. The creature let out a haunting howl that echoed throughout the forest, sending shivers down our spines.

Every second felt like an eternity as Todd scrambled to start the RV. The engine roared to life, and we quickly pulled away from our campsite. The rain was relentless, making it difficult to navigate the slippery trails, but Todd's firm grip on the steering wheel guided us.

The eerie howls of the creature continued, growing fainter as we distanced ourselves. But the image of that creature, standing tall with its menacing eyes, was etched in our minds. We drove in silence, the gravity of our encounter weighing heavily on us.

Hours seemed to pass before we finally felt safe enough to stop. Parking the RV at a well-lit rest stop, we tried to process what had just happened. "Do you think it was... Bigfoot?" I hesitated to voice the thought. Todd looked deep in thought. "I don't know, but whatever it was, it wasn't ordinary."

Sleep was elusive that night. Every noise, every rustle, set us on edge. We kept replaying the events, trying to make sense of the creature's presence. We remembered the tales we'd heard from the locals but had dismissed them as mere stories.

"I think we should cut our trip short," Todd murmured. I nodded in agreement. As much as we loved camping and the outdoors, this experience had shaken us to our core. The allure of nature had been tainted by the unknown.

As dawn broke, we continued our journey back to the RV rental place. The picturesque landscapes we had admired during our trip now seemed overshadowed by an uneasy feeling, knowing that something mysterious lurked within.

The rental place was bustling with activity when we arrived. Families were picking up RVs, excitedly talking about their planned adventures. Little did they know of the mysteries that lay hidden in the vastness of the forests.

As we handed over the keys, the salesman noticed our disheveled appearance and quizzically raised an eyebrow. "Rough trip?" he joked. Before we could reply, he added, "If you enjoyed the RV, we're selling some new ones. Interested?"

Todd and I exchanged a knowing look. The memories of our encounter were still fresh. "No, thank you," we said in unison. As we left the rental place, we silently vowed to take a break from camping for a while. Some mysteries, we realized, were best left undiscovered.

Conclusion

In concluding, the myriad tales of Bigfoot encounters in Oregon paint a captivating mosaic of a creature that perennially slips through our fingers. The narratives in this book, gathered from diverse regions of the state, manifest a remarkable consistency in their depiction of this elusive being, its features, and the deep impression it leaves on those fortunate—or perhaps unfortunate enough—to cross its path.

However, these tales are not merely figments of the imagination, springing from the abyss of the unknown. They invite us to accept that even our most traversed territories might be hiding secrets, potentially nestled within the lesser-known recesses of our beloved state. These Oregon Bigfoot tales beckon us to consider whether our scenic backdrops might shroud mysteries deeper than we've previously fathomed. As our journey into scientific exploration continues to deepen, it's crucial to engage with these enduring enigmas with both an open heart and a sharp mind, as it's within these veiled crevices that authentic discoveries await.

What do these accounts mean for Oregonians and all who journey through its varied terrains? They spark a revitalized sense of awe and expectation, nurtured by the notion that mysterious beings could be dwelling among us, expertly evading our sight for ages. They suggest that Oregon's lush forests and expansive valleys could still hold tales eager for their moment in the spotlight.

While skepticism towards these tales is natural, given that exceptional claims require exceptional proof, it's vital that our doubts don't diminish our inherent wonder and passion for unearthing realities. The ongoing dialogue about Bigfoot's existence encapsulates the human spirit's innate inquisitiveness and our unyielding pursuit of understanding. It's paramount that we don't let biases hinder our journey towards genuine enlightenment.

As you meander through Oregon's natural wonders, be it for brief instances or extended escapades, indulge in the thought that you're treading lands steeped in local legends. Remain alert and open to the possibility of facing the enigmatic.

No matter where one stands on the real existence of Bigfoot, the testimonies from those wholly convinced of their encounters emanate a compelling message: our cosmos is brimming with undiscovered wonders, and welcoming these mysteries can deeply enhance our existence. May the tales of Bigfoot encounters in Oregon ignite within you an unquenchable curiosity and a dedication to unraveling nature's intricate web. Who knows what tales Oregon's forests are eager to unveil?

As this book reaches its conclusion and you ponder its numerous accounts, recognize that the true magnetism of these stories is not solely in the conclusions they offer, but in the reflection they provoke. It's this intense reflection that lights the path of exploration, leading us closer to the marvels surrounding us. Thus, in your future treks across Oregon's expansive wilderness, maintain a watchful eye and a brave heart—you might just stumble upon the remarkable.

Printed in Great Britain
by Amazon